Also by Rob Smith:

Night Voices
The Spell of Twelve

Rob Smith

CHILDREN OF LIGHT

Drinian Press/
Huron, Ohio

Children of Light

Library of Congress Control Number: 2006903729

ISBN 0-9785165-2-4

Rob Smith

CHILDREN OF LIGHT

With you are the fountains of life;
In your light we see light.

Tehillim 36:9

CHILDREN OF LIGHT

1

Orfin and Borthid were trembling as they approached the rendezvous point. They were well aware that the initial contact with interplanetary species was a delicate arrangement requiring diplomatic skills, and theirs were not yet tested. All during the last month of their voyage, they practiced the removal of the "R" sound from their earth speech, or rather "eeth" speech. In practice, however, they would slip. It was always the simplest of mistakes. Orfin would navigate complex sentences, and fail when asked his own name. "Oefin" he would repeat, after Borthid's smiling glance would tell him that he had done it again.

Now, everything depended upon not slipping. The interplanetary protocol readout clearly stated that the

Photosynthoids should be treated with the utmost caution. Every query regarding the Photosynthoids told them that a slip of the tongue, or rather the roll of an "R", would provide the ultimate indignity, and could arouse them to violence. They opted to begin their interaction by writing down every response, and reading a peculiar dialect of their own language minus the "R's".

The transporter pod came to a stop. It had covered the forty-five kilometers from the docking point of the ship in about four minutes. A distinctly terran voice spoke as the portal opened. "This is the embackation point. You will be geeted by the cuewent ambassidoe at the end of the passage. You may encountoo Photosynthoids enwoute. Please weefane fum vocal communications until following you beefing."

The two were not prepared for what their eyes saw. While they had seen holograms of the Photosynthoids, the scale had eluded them. Here, along the blindingly bright corridor, stood a trio of the green hulking shapes. Roughly speaking, they appeared humanoid, bi-pedal, erect, and having two arms, but there the similarity stopped. They had a webbed neck and walked in a more apelike manner, exposing their extra back flap of skin to the overhead light. There was no escaping the alarming appearance of their green skin though the palmed surface of their webbed fingers was red to orange in hue. Without saying a word, Borthid and Orfin exchanged glances. Beyond that, the air inside the corridor was remarkably fresh, if not intoxicating, and the two began to believe the propaganda that had sent them off as voyagers across the universe in search of Galcon, the very first inhabited planet known to terrans.

"Geetings, fellow tavelees," came a lighthearted voice from the left. They turned to see a round-faced man in dark glasses. They took him to be in his forties. He smiled, and extended his hand as he approached. "I see you made it quite safely! Please follow me."

He led them to a darkened corridor off the main passage. "I am Ambassador Costance," he said in a whisper. They glanced at each other hearing the "r" plainly spoken in his title. "We can be less guarded in our speech here," he said, as if anticipating a question. "They never come down this hallway. It's too dark."

Before they could follow up on his comment, a portal quietly opened, and they stepped over a threshold into a dimly lit room. Costance removed his glasses and walked over to a crystal decanter. "You are probably hungry, and tired of ship's fare," he announced. "All you'll find on this planet is *longstol*. You'll tire of it quickly enough, yet the first draft is quite satisfying." He poured out three vials of a thick golden syrup and, keeping one for himself, offered one to Borthid and one to Orfin. "Cheers," he said raising the glass, "Or should I use the local parlance, 'Cheese'?" He laughed at his own cleverness and sipped at the viscous liquid. "Sip it slowly," he added, "it can be quite heady."

The two raised their glasses and took a sip. The drink (or was it a food?) was both hot and cold with a marvelous sweetness that could only be described as "comforting". The three sat silent, as though in the midst of a sacred ritual. Costance seemed more ready to end the repast, and broke the silence with a smacking of his lips. "I'd love something solid to eat, after being here two month... but, there is something about this *longstol*." Orfin and Borthid could only bring themselves to nod in agreement.

"So you're the lucky lottery winners," stated the Ambassador. "How are you enjoying your prize so far?"

"It has been incredible!" blurted out Borthid. "Nine months ago we were headed nowhere, and now we're half way across the stars!" Costance eyed her in such a way that she felt obligated to continue. "I mean, I did well enough in school, but I'm a discontinued model, and feared that my only option would be as a childer."

"I can see that you both are discontinued models," remarked Costance, "but now the lottery has made you the envy of the world."

"I suppose it has," answered Orfin. "To be Citizen Explorers for a year is quite an adventure. I understand that the last pilots of our craft have actually been settled in a new colony."

"Yes," replied the Ambassador coolly. "The official record indicates that the last crew of the *Renegade* joined the cooperative on *Thanatos-IV*; it's in a newly-charted sector just being opened by The Council. Perhaps you will choose to join them at the conclusion of your tour."

"It will be sad to leave the *Renegade*," remarked Orfin, glancing at Borthid. "She's one of the Star-Gazer class, you know."

"With a four-phasing Ceretrak," added Costance, "It does have all the amenities for the pleasurable passage of time. I suppose that the lure of cortex stimulation is as much a part of the adventure as the urge to explore other worlds." Costance's eyes wandered down Borthid's physique. Her coveralls did not disguise the contours of her womanhood, nor did the ebony features of this discontinued model seem to cool his attraction to her. Orfin had the urge to step between them to cut off his hungry stare, but he held his seat. "Of course," continued the Ambassador, "I suppose, it's all relative. I've been honored with this duty, which carries its own pleasures. My companion is an

Alpha, and we will have a child when my term has ended. In our own way, each of us must do our part. Perhaps Borthid would consent to childing our embryo when your year has ended."

Orfin gritted his teeth. It was, of course, the natural order of things that the discontinued women were useful to society for carrying the implanted embryos of the more genetically robust, but his time aboard the ship had given him an affinity toward Borthid that he could not explain. If Borthid could not bear a child of her own, he resented that she should be endangered for the sole purpose of bearing the child of an *Alpha*.

"Yes," said Costance, "Vienna is an *Alpha*. Would you like to see her?" He did not wait for an answer, but fingered his wrist control, and a portal opened. Orfin assumed it led deeper into the Ambassador's chambers. A statuesque woman entered. She wore a deep blue metallic cat-suit that coated her taut flesh like a second skin. She glittered as she walked with only the slightest roll of her narrow hips. "Isn't she beautiful?" admired Costance.

Vienna seemed not to regard Borthid or Orfin but pleaded with the Ambassador, "Cosy, can we go now? It's nearly time, and I am past ready." The whine in her voice spoke an urgency not reflected in her vacant expression.

"In a moment, my Lovely," answered Costance. "Get the rings and I'll meet you at the observation lounge in time for the sixth phasing." He looked to his guests to gauge their reaction to his last words. Yes, he thought, they were impressed that their ship had a four-phase Ceretrak. His was an eight. He and Vienna were on a three-hour phasing program and in less than ten minutes he would be otherwise engaged with his *Alpha*.

"This station has an eight-phaser," he bragged. "It's a dirty job, but someone has to do it," he added, laughing to himself. "We've taken to going over to the lounge area when it's time. The Froggies, I mean, the Photosynthoids, make the air so light it heightens the effect. But you'll learn that soon enough." He rose to his feet.

Orfin protested, "But what about our briefing?"

"Later," replied Costance curtly. "A lady is in distress, and I'm the cure. Follow me to the lounge if you like. You can take a table there and have some more *longstol*, unless of course your Ceretrak has repowered and you have to return to the ship?" The two shook their heads. "I wouldn't think so," he added. "You'll be safe enough in the lounge. Don't talk to the locals, and mind your 'R's'," he added with a wink. "Sorry you can't join us," he said to the two of them, but Orfin saw that he was looking at Borthid, and his hungry stare had returned. With that, he was out of the room. Orfin and Borthid had to run to keep up with him, but even then they fell behind. They followed down the corridor which took a sudden sharp left turn and opened into a wide sunlit mall. They came up short in the expansive arena, blinking in the brightness of its light. Photosynthoids were walking freely about, but Ambassador Costance was nowhere to be seen.

2

Like the earth, Galcon is a place of great blue heavens and huge white clouds. The similar colors in the sky are largely due to the gaseous similarities of the atmosphere. That, however, is where the resemblance ends. By earth standards, the topography is bleak at best. On the surface at least, it appears to be a desert and barren of all life.

More than the land, however, the atmosphere proved to be the exciting find. There was quite an uproar when its image appeared as a computer-enhanced smudge from a deep space probe. At first, the analysts could not see it as a planet at all. One scientist referred to it as a "cosmic burp" since it appeared to be a gas bubble trapped in a swirling mass between the gravitational pull of two small stars in the Milton Cluster.

The space charters dubbed it "the Oasis" since it looked like a place where ships could siphon off fresh oxygen to remain in space for longer periods of time. The tabloids popularized the discovery by calling it "the Truck Stop" while renowned theorists adopted numerous models to explain both the possibility and impossibility of its existence. In the end, the politicians decided to settle the matter by sending a manned probe. Of course, the wisdom of sending a human was contested by the scientific community. Such an action posed a clear danger to life when a sensor probe would accomplish the same thing. The Planetary Council had other designs, however. The population was bored with data from collecting machines. A high profile adventure and a new hero would do much to calm down a restless citizenry.

The plan for the voyage was turned over to the space charters. Their initial excitement over the realization that the interplanetary distance could be covered in a short time was dampened by the fact that the return would be nearly impossible, at least not in a human lifetime. It was explained that a travel window was opened by the present planetary alignments. By using solar winds and "slingshotting" around gravitational fields, the outward journey was downhill all the way. There was a major problem, however. The boomerang effect that could propel a lightweight craft to its destination in a matter of months would not become favorable for a return in less than 780 years.

In that time, the solar system alignments would change, thus opening the travel window in the opposite direction.

Dr. David Jahren was eloquent before the Planetary Council in its closed meeting. He presented the supplementary documents to prove the case for both the "quick out" and the problematic return. He also showed the case for another option. The return was theoretically possible if made by a thin-skinned, non-metallic craft. The plan was called the "subway" because, while it could guarantee the return of the ship, it could not protect the crew or passengers. The "subway" was a way that ships could be recycled, but it was not survivable for life forms. The Council took interest in the possibilities and was ready to authorize funds to solve the survivability problem. Jahren explained that it was not a matter of money. The fact was that the thin-skin that would dissipate the heat encountered in the "subway" could not protect living tissue. In other words, the technology that made the quick return possible was not user-friendly.

The Council listened intently to all the arguments and received the computerized documentation that was submitted under Jahren's name. Unfortunately, the name of Dr. David Jahren also appeared on an accident report that same day. He was tragically killed in a vehicular mishap after leaving the presentation. His obituary was highlighted by an announcement that "Dr. David Jahren's extensive work has outlined the technology and requirements for safe space travel to and from the 'cosmic truck stop'. Named in honor of his achievement, the 'Jahren Project' is expected to be operational by the end of the current year."

Jahren's graduate assistant was appalled at the report. Sure that the Council had misunderstood the data, she called together the research team for a teleconference directly with the Planetary Council. A week later, the whole team perished when a turbo lift failed at the Center for Interplanetary Exploration (CIPE). Later that afternoon, an unknown environmental terrorist group calling themselves SUFFER claimed responsibility. The police confirmed that sabotage had been the cause of the lift failure, and the details matched those described by the caller from the organization to Save the Universe from Future Earth Refuse. The case was considered closed. In tribute to the loss of the young scientists, the Council agreed that the first production craft to make the journey to Galcon would be called *The Young Martyrs*.

3

Borthid and Orfin were on the edge of panic as they found themselves alone in the great open space of the pavilion. In truth, they could hardly be considered alone. In the large mall were about a dozen of the strange beings that they had been taught to call Photosynthoids. Before they could catch their breath, they realized that the eight-foot-tall green creatures were moving toward them.

Borthid felt her stomach roll when she realized that they were surrounded. Every lesson that they had taken regarding language contacts left her. She wanted to scream as she felt the touch of someone next to her. She turned to see Orfin, and the fear that was in his face matched her own. "We signed up to come, didn't we?" he asked rhetorically. A wave of relief washed over both of them. Borthid wondered if his spoken sentence meant that he could communicate with these odd beings, or whether he was just lucky to speak a sentence without any "R's".

Their private fears proved ungrounded when they realized that no hands were reaching out to take them captive. Afraid to speak, it occurred to them both that the Photosynthoids were not after them, but after the richness of the carbon dioxide that they expelled from their nostrils. Orfin felt a strange feeling come over him, one he could not describe. In that moment of silence, he sensed a oneness with his companion of nine months. He turned to Borthid who met his gaze. In later days, the two would remember this moment, but would ascribe its magic, at least in part, to the oxygen-rich presence of this alien race.

"Evie one, clea away," called out a voice from the crowd, "These awe new to Galcon. We must leave them alone."

At first the two thought the ambassador had come to their rescue, but the voice came from the crowd of Photosynthoids. The command was followed by a jumble of responses, and the cluster of aliens seemed to dissolve around them. Orfin and Borthid would like to have thanked their deliverer, but no one stepped forward. They also could not tell if anyone was looking at them. This was the first time that they considered that the Photosynthoids had no discernable eyeballs. What they had taken as eyes from a distance were more like red spots of coloration on the sides of their heads. Borthid, who was a student of biology, thought that they were akin to "eye spots" in some invertebrates. She could not guess how much they could actually see. Certainly they had no "normal" focusing ability and probably no stereovision, since the spots were located on the sides of their heads and not facing forward. Once she realized this, she understood the strangeness of their gaits. They rolled their heads from side to side, probably to gain some sense of depth and distance. Because their eyes had no pupils, she could not tell the direction of their focus, if any.

The Photosynthoids took positions on crystal divans around the room. Borthid's and Orfin's disorientation was not entirely due to the presence of other life forms. The lighting was also very strange. At first, they could not put their fingers on the difference. Orfin was first to recognize it. "There are no shadows," he said in an excited whisper.

"Shhh!" was her quick reply. "Watch you speech! Follow me", she commanded. She led him to one of the more remote crystalline couches. She sat down on the edge of it, and was surprised to find that it was neither hard nor cool. "This is not like any stone on earth!" she observed.

It was Orfin's turn to remind her of her speech. "Eeth," he corrected.

"I think it will be alright to talk here if we keep our voices down," she pleaded. "Look at this." She pointed at a low bench. "It's glowing!" She was right. The seat was also a light source. In fact, everything in the room emanated light. Walls, ceiling, floor, every aspect of the room's interior was a light source.

"It's like we're inside a diamond," Orfin observed. The difference between objects and forms was not identified by shadow, but by color, and there seemed to be no beams or supports, unless they, too, were luminescent. Even to their untrained eyes, it was apparent to Borthid and Orfin that they were looking at an unknown technology; or rather they were "inside" an unknown technology.

They turned to each other in silence, and had a startling realization. They had been continuous companions for the last nine earth months, yet they had not really seen each other. Here in the shadowless light of Galcon they could see each other as they were. More than that, they also were able to see each other freshly, well away from the culture that had labeled them "discontinued models". There was a beauty about them both that defied their crossbreed status on earth. Borthid, whose wide hips would allow her to bear the surrogate children of the *Alphas*, wore the skin tones of an African-European mulatto. It was a distinction that would keep her genetic material out of the master plan for planetary population. Orfin, too, would not participate in the future generation. His Native American features clearly masked the Chinese line that arrived in the North American west during the building of the first transcontinental railway. The two had their lives dramatically changed when they won the lottery to become Citizen Explorers and found themselves thrown together in a small craft with a four-phasing

Ceretrak and the possibility of escaping the inevitable futures that waited them on earth. Had she stayed, Borthid would have become a part of the "baby factory". It was a status which she would have accepted as a consolation for the fact that she could never have children of her own. Like Orfin, she was rendered sterile by the virus that touched those of mixed race. She remembered the compassion of the state physician when she was given the news. She consoled herself with the fact that she was not alone. Millions, in those years, found out that they would never have children. It was an act of God that they would be the "discontinued models" who would be given the privilege of birthing the future through embryonic implants. The men, like Orfin, had no such consolation. They could bear no children, and neither would they father them. They became the worker eunuchs. Some by their prowess became star athletes. Rumor had it that their being "less male" in some ways made them "more male" in others. Orfin did not fit the stereotype. A poet at heart, he struggled for meaning in a world that offered little to anyone, and none to him. Here on Galcon, looking into Borthid's eyes, what they had been seemed long past. In the light of this strange place, the shadows of the mind also vanished in the even illumination of the environment.

Suddenly their trancelike gaze was shattered by loud, breathy shrieks. It was a woman's voice, wild and unbounded. The sound was startling, at first, and fear gripped the two. The frenetic sounds soon shifted to sighs and they understood what they were hearing. The phasing cycle had come to an end, and it had unleashed the usual waves of endorphins that were the reward of the cortex stimulation of the Ceretrak. Probably it was Vienna, caught in the delight of the Ambassador's eight-phaser.

4

The exploration of space brought many developments to benefit humankind. It also brought economic boon to those corporations that had the good fortune to be able to adopt the technology of space to an acceptable addiction of the general population.

Video games and home computer shopping paled in comparison to the introduction of C-tunes in the early twenty-first century. The ability to provide direct stimulation to the cerebral cortex was revolutionary. It also began a series of societal changes that could not have been imagined by its promoters. The first experiments were meant simply to bypass consumer protests against commercial advertising. They came in the form of ring tones which could be freely downloaded for cell phones. At first these carried simple subliminal messages that promoted soft drinks and motion pictures.

Some criticized the initiative on several levels. Ethicists argued that subliminal advertising had long been restricted on the moral grounds that it eliminated personal choice. The counter to that claim, however, carried the day. Because the ring tones were freely added by the consumer who gladly downloaded them, the right of the public to choose was held intact.

No one could argue with the results. When a cola company first set its plan in motion, every can and bottle disappeared from every shelf in the test market, while their competitors' products gathered dust. Weekend box office records fell to a low budget b-film when crowds lined up for blocks to see it over and over.

At first brain physiologists were stymied by the outcome. In an effort to understand the effect, they postulated that the c-tunes were providing direct cortex stimulation, bypassing conscious thought. As they proceeded with their scientific caution, cell phone manufacturers improved their designs so that the appliance could be worn at all times.

As it turned out, the first experience was somewhat of a fluke. Other c-tunes did not fully measure up to the commercial success of the first encounter. Still, they were effective enough to change the world of advertising.

As the phenomenon was studied, however, the neuro-mechanism was identified. The project was classified, but research was continued by the space administration. The neurological affect was seen as a potential solution to a problem that had nagged the agency for generations. "How do you sustain a deep space crew in the course of unavoidable boredom, heightened stress, and prolonged passages?"

The new technology held a lot of potential. If direct cerebral stimulation could create the psychological equivalent of a day at the beach or a night at the theater, it would provide an effective remedy to boredom, fatigue, and fear.

Once isolated, technology to stimulate the brain was easily adapted from commercially available cell phones. The problem was limiting its use. Early experiments with rats showed that the animals would literally starve to death while continually depressing a control lever to release brain stimulation. Space travelers would have to be given a rationed use of brain stimulation if any work or observation was expected of them. The final product was the Ceretrak 500, which would allow two space travelers to enjoy phases every six hours, four times in a cycle.

In the early days, the expanded technology was kept strictly secret. The fear was that there would be a public uproar if it were known that the heroes of planetary space research had replaced a night's sleep with half hour uninterrupted pleasure from direct cortex stimulation. In point of fact, the crews were quickly addicted to the cerebral distractions that the machine was capable of creating. The Neptune Project disaster, that cost the lives of four explorers, was officially credited to an airlock malfunction. Those on the inside of the project, however, knew the truth. Within three days of launch, the four travelers were so addicted to the Ceretrak that the crew members murdered each other. The device was set to provide "watches" with two crew members on duty while the others took "sleep period" (as it was explained to the public).

The first murders were carefully premeditated to take place during a meteor storm that temporarily cut communications with the earth. It took place when the on-duty crew members murdered their partners during a phasing. The third murder took place when one of the two surviving crew members improperly hooked himself up to the Ceretrak and feigned his stimulation until his partner was too deeply gone to resist him. For the final crew member, his remorseless reward was sixteen couplings with the Ceretrak during each cycle.

When communication to earth was restored, the earth-stationed trackers were appalled. The survivor reported that he had killed the others in self-defense, claiming that the failure of his own Ceretrak had saved his life. As he explained it, he had just entered his rest period when the two on-duty pilots killed his watch mate. When they turned on him, he was able to fight them off. This, at least, was born out by the on-board computer that showed that only one traveler had logged on at the last phasing.

The three bodies were jettisoned through the airlock. The flight psychologists at the command center prescribed full use of the Ceretrak as the "best drug" to treat the shock of the sole survivor. For three cycles, sixteen times a cycle, the remaining traveler enjoyed an uninterrupted sequence of rewards for his grizzly labor. In the end, the ship was lost when its solo pilot ignored warning systems, rather than miss a phasing when the machine had repowered. The official report cited the computer records that showed the unscheduled operation of the airlock. Engineers and designers were diverted to investigate whether such an occurrence was a human error, or a design flaw. The final verdict was human error. The airlock had been inadvertently activated with the loss of three lives, leaving one crew member who could not control the ship single-handedly.

The investigation was closed and a memorial to the lost crew was established at the International Space Exploration Museum.

Those who were privy to the truth were elated. Mission Control had opened Pandora's Box and was enamored by the power that had been unleashed. The new assignment became the control of the addiction in a way that could further a mission and the productivity of a crew. Multiple safeguards were set in place, and these principles proved themselves on subsequent missions. The new procedures required that the entire crew had to enter the phasing mode at the same time, and the sensing units were interrelated so as not to operate independently. Individual control codes and access numbers were assigned to each crew member, and no phasings could begin until all had logged on. Crew efficiency was improved by linking the recycling to the on-board computers' operational "checklist". No phasings could occur until all the housekeeping tasks were done and the ship was secure for automatic cruising for the duration of the crew's "sleep period". Finally, remote sensors would allow Mission Control the ability to disable the Ceretrak from earth, the ultimate threat to an addicted crew.

Rumors of the development of the Ceretrak began to filter out, and eventually, the members of the Planetary Council were admitted into the ring of those who knew about the machine.

For some, it was an amusing tidbit, at least until they experienced it first hand. The first unit known to be installed outside a space research facility or craft was in the headquarters of the Planetary Council. Soon after, funds for developing low cost "home units" were approved. This was all done without much thought to a wider market. For the most part, the Council members thought of their use as a part of the privilege of the ruling class of professional diplomats who were, they told themselves, the equivalent to the flight crew of spaceship earth.

Blane Wallerton saw more than the others. He and Mirabella Quan laid out plans for a more widely-marketed approach. They decided to market the product under the name used by the Space Exploration Council, the "Ceretrak 500". It was promoted as a self-help device to bring inner peace and achieve the full power of the senses. For Quan and Wallerton, the foremost world leaders, there was the insight that the Ceretrak 500 could do so much more. They knew that the real benefits would fall to those who controlled its distribution. Quietly, they applied for the rights to assign the millifrequencies that would be required for the widespread use of the Ceretrak 500. In their marketing campaign, they called it "a marvel for humanity, born of the exploration of space".

5

The Photosynthoids did not seem to acknowledge the piercing cries of ecstasy that filled the brightly lit atrium. Orfin and Borthid could not conceal their amusement. The ambassador had taken such pride in introducing Vienna. It was certainly status for the round-faced Costance to be seen with her, but it was equally apparent that what she saw in him was access to an eight-phaser. Her loud abandon in this alien world showed that she enjoyed the physical reactions to the Ceretrak much more than his company. He relished in the status of being paired to an *Alpha*, and she in the fact that his access to technology turned the key to her only pleasure. His smugness could not be camouflaged when he reappeared in the sunlit room.

"There you are," he called out to the couple as they huddled together. "That was refreshing. Could you hear Vienna?" Borthid and Orfin could not tell whether he was asking or bragging.

"We heard," offered Borthid, after a pause.

"She does like having me as her phasing partner," responded the Ambassador. "Am I speaking too crassly, my dear?" he asked, looking at Borthid. Orfin rose to his feet. "No need for gallantries, young man," corrected Costance, gesturing that Orfin sit down. "You are on my planet now, and I'm sure you would not want to deny your ship's partner the opportunity to experience the full range of pleasure that my humble office has to offer?" He licked his lips as Borthid turned her face away to avoid his eyes.

"May I suv you and you guests, Ambassadoe?" came a soft, breathy voice from behind. Borthid and Orfin turned to see a Photosynthoid speaking, its red eye-spot generally directed to Costance.

"Yes, Bog-kin," replied Costance. "Bing us *longstol*. I need a bit of sustenance, and take some to the *Alpha*." The green humanoid bowed, turned, and shuffled off. "The Froggies are really strange," whispered the ambassador. "They don't have names, you know. Whatever you call them, they'll respond. I call them all 'Bog-kin'. I told them it's a name of honor, but in truth, it has no 'R's' and they look like they are related to something from a bog." He laughed at his own cleverness, but he laughed alone. "I'll give them this," he said, breaking the awkward silence that followed the break in his snickering, "they learned terran speech quickly enough. The first team taught them a phonetic alphabet and gave them a dictionary. The syntax followed right along. If you correct their grammar, they never make the mistake again, and it's all of them. It's like if you tell one, the others know it too."

"How do you explain that?" questioned Orfin, whose curiosity was peaked.

"We aren't sure," continued Costance. "They are a simple species. They have no need for food gathering, no natural enemies that we can determine, and no technology."

"No technology?" queried Borthid. "What do you call this structure we're sitting in?"

"I call it a cave," came the answer. "It appears to be a hollow crystal. I know that some of them move in and out of it, but I have yet to find a portal, other than the ship docking port. Further, no one can tell me how this was made or how long it's been here. I think it's a naturally occurring structure that suits our purposes very well."

"And what are our purposes?" asked Orfin, not hiding the disapproval in his voice. Costance turned to him coldly.

"Our purpose is to determine the suitability of this planet for a colony, to chart its resources, and assess the strength of the indigenous population. Your purpose, Citizen Explorer, is to report to your Ambassador and do as you're told." Costance's face flushed red and his green eyes flashed out at what he considered impertinence.

"He awe you dinks," came the raspy voice of a Photosynthoid

who set down three glasses in front of the humans.

"Thank you, Bog-kin" was the Ambassador's imperious reply. Borthid looked at the alien. She was not sure that the creature who now humbly bowed and backed away was the same one whom they had seen a few moments before. She puzzled why she should know that. Was it a differentiation of features? No, she mused it was a difference in scent. The earlier Photosynthoid had a lighter aroma. This one was, she reflected, more humid. She glanced quickly at the Ambassador and Orfin, but they were locked in the tension of their exchange and did not notice. She reached for her glass. It was very heavy in her hand, not at all like the polyplastics of the space craft. She sipped the rich liquid which seemed to warm her all over. The voices of Orfin and Costance seemed to be far off as her eyes rolled around the large room. Whether it was the *longstol* or a heightened awareness, she began to sense that the room was not as it had seemed. What had seemed a large open expanse was suddenly shrouded in thick mists as if the dome had become a dense cloud chamber, and through it streaked salvoes of light as startlingly bright as they were silent. Then it seemed like the lights converged to become one. "Who are you?" she called out, but the only answer was Orfin, shaking her arm and calling her name.

"Borthid! Borthid, are you alright?"

The smoke cleared and the room returned to what it had been, a sunny pavilon with a scattering of green bi-peds scuttering about.

"It must be that the *longstol* is too heady for her," came the Ambassador's voice. "You'd best get her back to the ship. By my calculation, you are due to repower in a few moments. The sleep phasing should pull her back to reality."

Orfin was surprised at Costance's awareness of his ship's Ceretrak recycling mode. Orfin had almost forgotten, but the Ambassador seemed deeply aware of such things. Of course, thought Orfin, Vienna's reaction might have sharpened his sense of it all. He rose to his feet and offered his arm to Borthid.

"That's it," counseled Costance, "take her through a phasing and that'll put reality back in her." He called to a Photosynthoid nearby, "Bog-kin, help them find the passage to the ship." A fawning creature bowed toward him and shuffled along side Borthid, on the opposite arm from Orfin.

They had gone no farther than out of earshot from Costance when Borthid spoke. Her voice stopped Orfin cold. "I'm not going to the ship."

Orfin did not understand the comment, but could not doubt the conviction behind it. "What?" he said.

"I am not going back to the ship," she repeated.

"But it's weepowed," protested Orfin who looked nervously at the hulking green shape across from him, hoping that Borthid would remember to modify her speech.

"Mother," she said. Orfin's breath stopped within him. He looked for a reaction from the Photosynthoid. Borthid raised her voice at him, "Mother... my access code is M-O-T-H-E-R. Take the *Alpha* with you if you must keep the phasing!" She had violated the code of speech. She pulled herself free from him, and to his surprise, she addressed the Photosynthoid, "I know who you are," she stated clearly. "Will you take me to the high place?"

In a clear human voice the green creature said, "Yes, Chosen One," and then they were gone.

Orfin stood alone, and the light around him seemed suddenly chill.

6

Behind the headlines and the people who made history, Blane Wallerton and Mirabella Quan reconstructed the culture of the planet. They had quietly bought up the rights to the millifrequencies that made the Ceretrak 500 available to the mass market. The technology was simple, and their creativity was in seeing the possibilities. On the Planetary Council, they had been the fiercest of competitors, each striving to put together coalitions to undercut the domination of the other.

They had both been present when the space agency presented the first briefing to the council, and it was perhaps only luck that found them together on the executive turbo lift that same afternoon. Usually surrounded by an entourage, they had separately retreated to try to bring some perspective to what they had just seen and experienced. In the lift they stole glances, each trying to penetrate the consciousness of the other as if to anticipate the next move in a grand game.

"You know what it means, don't you?" asked Mirabella, breaking the seething silence of close proximity.

"Yes," was the simple reply. "What do you propose?" he asked.

"A planetary majority of two," was her cryptic response. The message was clear to Blane Wallerton who only nodded his agreement. His silent response served to foil the guards and reporters who regularly eavesdropped in on turbo lift conversations.

Wallerton pulled out a pen and wrote on his palm: "QR-6, 4:00". He held his hand out to her. She saw the message, and accepted his handshake for the sake of the security camera.

"Alone! No tricks!" he added.

"Agreed!" she answered, stepping off the lift at her office suite level. They each felt a surge of adrenalin, as they returned to what now seemed the mundane work of running a planet. At 4:00 in Quiet Room 6, they would either take over the world together, or destroy each other trying. Wallerton rubbed his palms together until the ink smeared to illegibility.

At 4:00 they met in the corridor outside the sixth floor quiet room. They did not speak until after they had entered the electronically-protected chamber. The room was dominated by a heavy conference table and plush upholstered wing chairs. Neither was willing to sit as long as the other was standing. In this game, the spoils went to the strong, and Mirabella Quan was not going to give up her height advantage by being seated.

Wallerton started to run his identity card through the magnetic strip reader when Quan gestured him off. She activated the system off her own card, carefully entering her pin number when the readout monitor prompted her. When the white noise whirring reached its pitch, she held the card up and spoke. "I got this from an aide. When they review the access codes, they'll be no record we were here."

Blane Wallerton beamed at her. "Great minds, and all that!"

he said holding up his own bogus card. "How did you get the access code?" he asked.

"My people do what I tell them," was her reply. "The perks I offer are too good to lose." Her words carried a tone of cold passion that aroused Wallerton who licked his fat lips.

"I'll bet we'd both enjoy exchanging perks. We've been competitors too long. Maybe it's time to consummate an alliance?"

"You make it sound like we're going to seal this deal in bed," she observed. "Aren't you afraid that I'm the black widow who devours her mate?"

"I can be ravenous, too! Let's face it, two insatiable people might find a lot of ways to be amused, and in ways more potent than the space agency's cerebral stimulations. That's what we're here to discuss, right?"

"Right!" agreed Mirabella. "That thing has gigantic political potential."

"Especially to those who resist using it," added Wallerton.

"Then you do understand," observed Quan. "That thing may be the most addicting device ever. It has to be controlled, or people will plug themselves in until they starve to death."

"Like rats in an experiment that can't stop pushing a button that releases brain endorphins," said Wallerton. "I figure that usage has to be rationed to prevent overuse. Otherwise, it appears to be a 'drug' with no side effects. There's no residual stupor or bodily deterioration. The people who phase together are totally oblivious to each other. They will be totally isolated, and their whole world will be encased in tiny cavity of their puny skulls."

"How boring," put in Mirabella with a sly grin.

"But how perfect for the ones who control the frequency of use," observed Blane Wallerton.

"The word *control* is so harsh. I'm sure what you mean is that we can provide 'incentives for those who demonstrate loyalty and proficiency for the good of the planet!'" said Quan with a wink.

"Well, Mirabella, I'm sorry to point out that you just inadvertently used the word *we* when you talked about those who could offer incentives for loyalty. Sounds like we're working together for a change," asserted Wallerton. "Is the planet ready for this?"

"Why do you think my word choice was inadvertent? The planet may not be ready, but I am," whispered Quan. "Who gives a damn about the planet? Why shouldn't the two most powerful people have the most say? It's the law of the jungle." The two began to feel a rush, and as their words slowed, their desire heightened. At last silence took over, as if they were sizing each other up for the first time.

Wallerton broke the silence. "Just how insatiable are you?"

"Why not see for yourself?" she instructed. Mirabella backed to the edge of the conference table and, without breaking eye contact, pulled her skirt up over her hips and leaned back against the hard surface. She wore no undergarments. Wallerton lowered his gaze to see Quan's nakedness. "I'm always ready," she breathed. Blane dropped to his knees, and she guided his head to her waiting flesh.

A flurry of passion broke out as they tore at each other's clothes. Quan drew blood as she bit into the flesh of Wallerton's shoulder. He yelped and pulled back in pain. "That's so you won't ever forget that I am a black widow," she commanded. His response was to push her down and to slam himself into her with a ferocity that she had not anticipated. They climaxed abruptly; their passions still raging.

7

Orfin was at a loss. Being alone was the story of his life. When he had gone before the Nomenclator to declare his name, he had chosen *Orfin* as a thinly veiled alternative to *orphan*.

That's what he was, or at least what he felt like. His father had deserted his mother shortly after he was born, and she had died before his fifteenth birthday. When the virus had done its work on his body and he had been rendered sterile, he was declared a "discontinued model". He was a man without a father, and a man who would not be a father. Along with the millions of *Discontinueds*, he was issued a number to replace his family surname. If it all seemed too impersonal, it was a necessary part of a plan to track the progress of the viral infection. His number was related to a genetic key that linked him to others, the nameless faces that shared his ill-fated genetic heritage. As consolation, the Planetary Council offered new names and increased access to the Ceretraks.

Names among the *Discontinueds* were the subject of much speculation. People chose all sorts of titles and variations, all with the hope that one word could provide them with a sense of unique identity. It was a way to redefine the self. It took only an appointment with the government-appointed Nomenclator who verified the change and made its correlation with the genetic identity number. At birth, Orfin was named Paul Sanchez. "Sanchez" was his mother's name. "Paul" was the name of the father he never knew. When he was diagnosed, he accepted the offer of a name change, and avoided the "baby-book" variety names and the trendy variations that were becoming popular with others. *Orfin* was the name he chose. He stayed with it over the years. He avoided the temptation to change it as fashion permitted, not because of the money for the registration change, but because he did not want a number to be the most enduring aspect of his life's identity. Until he met Borthid, he had never known anyone who felt as he did. She had watched her mother become a baby-factory for the embryos of the wealthy. When the virus struck her family, it took mother and daughter. While the womb would not create its own embryo, it could nourish the implants from the *Alphas*, who found it convenient to have children without weight gain or stretch marks. She watched her mother's belly distend year after year, bearing children who were not her siblings. She also watched her mother's spirit die slowly as the babies invisibly passed through her body and into the world of the overindulged. Her mother lived for her visits to the Ceretrak. Her ration was once daily. It was increased to twice a day when she was under contract to do a birthing. Consequently, she was always pregnant or soon to be so, that is, until she was decertified. Her last child was born with Down's syndrome, and though it disappeared as cleanly as all the others, her subsequent contracts were cancelled. In response to her mother's depression, Borthid gave her mother her access card and the code to her Ceretrak. Borthid always wondered about the Down's baby. The birthing agency never divulged anything, and Borthid chose to believe that compassionate *Alphas* took the child to heart. Rumors were that such children were attached to neo-natal Ceretraks and allowed to starve.

Borthid had cried when she told Orfin the story, and she swore him to secrecy. That was during the hours of their space voyage together. Before that, they were strangers thrown together by the luck of the draw, winners in a lottery that gave them the title *Citizen Explorers*. For Orfin, the designation was a ticket to adventure in a life that was going nowhere. He sensed in Borthid, however, another purpose. If she was conscious of it, she never divulged it. It was more her manner that told him that she was moving toward something while he was running from something. The further they moved from the pull of earth's gravity, the freer she became. It surprised him when she began to hum as the two did the sail maneuvers that adjusted their course to catch the cosmic winds. By the seventh day, she was singing aloud. They were songs he did not know, but followed a melodic structure that was enhanced by the lack of instrumentation, rather than defeated by it. To his surprise, Orfin found himself humming along. Borthid never commented. She just looked at him and grinned as the two turned the giant winches that sheeted in the Mylar sails. Until now, Orfin was not aware of his dependence on her mood for his stability, but now that Borthid was gone, his options were limited.

He sat in the small cabin of his space craft. In front of him on the nav station table were the wrist rings of the ship's Ceretrak. The green LED's were flashing, indicating a full charge. He thought about slipping one on each hand and entering the security codes. It would be a way to escape, but it would also take away precious moments when he could be seeking Borthid. She might need his help; he had to think. She did not seem to be afraid of the Photosynthoids. She asked them to take her to the *high place*. Perhaps the ambassador would know where that was. He reached over and tapped the wrist rings to power down the Ceretrak. "That's a first", he thought. No one who knew him would ever believe that he would pass up a phasing; he could not believe it himself. He took a deep breath as he left the craft and plunged back into the corridor in search of Costance.

8

Orfin met Costance as he emerged from the darkened shaft that led to the Ambassador's quarters.

"You powered down your Ceretrak," was the Ambassador's greeting. "Are you crazy?"

"Borthid has been taken!" Orfin contested.

"I told you the Froggies are dangerous," chastised Costance. "Let's go to my chamber where we can talk." He turned and headed back down the corridor. Orfin followed.

Once inside, Costance poured out some *longstol* for Orfin, and a drink of something from a different cordial for himself. "Now tell me what happened," he said, handing the drink to Orfin. He gestured toward a seating area where they could both sit. They sat down, placing their drinks on the low table that was between them.

"Well, I was helping Borthid back to the ship, like you said, and one of the creatures spoke with her."

"Did she remember not to use R*'s*?" interrupted Costance.

"No, she didn't," he confessed. "The Photosynthoid used them too, and it spoke as plainly as you and I, not that sort of raspy croak," Orfin added.

Costance was beyond his own experience. He took a quick swig from his glass and drifted into deep concentration.

"Do you think they killed her?" said Orfin, with a shake in his voice.

The Ambassador looked up from his thought. "I doubt it, at least not outright. There's another purpose at work in these creatures. Can't you feel it?" He looked at Orfin who nodded. "They shuffle around like submissive apes, but they want something from us. Do you know what it is?" Orfin shook his head. "It's our carbon! That's why they're always sniffing our direction. They transform carbon dioxide to oxygen. They like our carbon dioxide. We're just *carbonators* to them. My guess is that they'll try to keep her breathing, even though she violated their code."

Orfin was trying to take it all in. It made sense, but not entirely. "But if they *need* our carbon dioxide, what did they do before we were here? I mean, it must be occurring naturally on this planet, or they couldn't have survived here."

"Now you're pushing it. There are some security issues that I can't betray," Costance stiffened.

"You mean, you know something, and won't tell me!" challenged Orfin. "Damn you! Borthid might be in danger." He was ready to leap across the table and take the fat man by the throat.

"Don't act noble with me," countered the Ambassador.

"You've lost your partner and can't access your Ceretrak. I know why you want her back. Face it, she's certainly not an *Alpha*."

Orfin was raging inside. But, while he was flushed with heat, his tone was cold as ice. "I have her access code. What I need is help, and you are going to give it to me!"

Costance's face flushed, but he contained his reaction. His voice was suddenly conciliatory, "Of course, you're concerned," he began, "your partner is in danger. I'm in a dilemma. I have classified information that may help you, but how do I know that you won't betray my trust if I divulge what I have been sworn to protect?"

Orfin could sense the progression of his logic. "How about if I were to offer some collateral?" he countered through gritted teeth.

"What do you have that I could possibly need?" challenged Costance with a patronizing tone.

"How about a functioning Ceretrak?" answered Orfin reaching into his pocket and pulling out the two wrist rings. He set them down on the low table.

The Ambassador sat up quickly. "With the access codes?" he queried.

"Yes, I'll give you the stupid codes, but first, you level with me!"

"Well," began Costance, settling in for a display of his superior knowledge, "you have to remember that this is highly classified information. If you breathe a word of it to anyone, your life will be forfeit, not to mention my diplomatic privilege."

"Get on with it," barked Orfin.

"You asked why they need our carbon dioxide when they have been here for so long. We do not believe that the Froggies are native to this place. In fact, we do not believe that this planet has been here for more than a few annual cycles. When this pocket of atmosphere was discovered, it was thought that it had been overlooked in previous deep space scans. When the computer records were reviewed, however, the astro scientists concluded that it wasn't *missed*. Rather, it wasn't *here*."

"You mean we're sitting in an air bubble that could pop at any second?" interrupted Orfin.

"It's not that critical. For those scientific types a short-lived bubble lasts at least a thousand years. That's why we have to be here. If we could stabilize the atmosphere, this could be a jump-off point for fifty generations of terrans. The problem is the Froggies. Where did they come from? We know they didn't evolve here. Either they arrived here before we did, and found that they could not maintain themselves here without finding a way to renew the carbon dioxide cycle, or..." The Ambassador's voice trailed off.

"Or what?" demanded Orfin.

"Or this *is* their space craft," said Costance in a low voice.

After a long silence, Orfin voiced his conclusions. "So if they are new to this planet, they may need us as *carbonators* the way we need them for oxygen. In that case, they'd keep us alive since there are only four of us."

"I'd say so," agreed Costance. "But they could replace us with rabbits, in the same way we could replace them with fresh vegetables."

"But if this thing is really the way they transport themselves," continued Orfin, "then it's a technology we can't begin to understand, and they probably have a way to make their own carbon dioxide. In which case, they really don't need us at all."

"Except as curiosities," offered Costance. "They do like our way of breathing. But note this: if we could find out how they operate this planet-ship... well, it could serve us as well as it serves them."

"Isn't that piracy?" asked a confused Orfin.

"Call it what you will," said Costance. "I'd say it's survival of the fittest. If they appear docile, it might just be their appearance. They do have Borthid. They also seem to be able to communicate with each other almost instantly. Remember I told you that if you correct the grammar of one, they all seem to know it?"

"Yes, I remember you saying that. But Borthid wasn't afraid of them. She asked to be taken to the *high place*. Do you know where that is?"

"No, I never heard of that place. In fact, movements around here are very restricted. That leads me to think that this may be a ship of sorts, and passages are sealed off or located in places where they are not recognizable. I've only been in the big atrium, and in the room where Vienna likes to use the eight-phaser." Costance quite literally blushed as he spoke the words. "She likes the high oxygen content," he added, and then with a low voice, "she likes it better than me." In the long silence that followed, Orfin began to understand Costance, or at least, to pity him.

"Maybe she'll appreciate this gift from you," Orfin said as he slid the wrist rings across the table. "Borthid's access code is 13-15-20-8-5-18 and mine is 1-12-15-14-5." He gave Costance the number codes, and did not speak the words from which they were derived. It was too personal, he thought, to tell him that a simple substitution of letters for numbers would spell *mother* and *alone*. The naming of those codes was between him and Borthid.

Orfin rose to his feet to leave.

"You know, I'm taking a risk," said Costance, "letting you live, that is." Orfin looked at him with disbelief. "If you find Borthid you'll want your Ceretrak back, but you'll not get it. If you get some information, though, I'll be able to get you anything you want... even an *Alpha.* We could both come out of this alright, but you've got to trust me."

"I'll keep you informed," Orfin pledged. "And I won't come back for those," he added, gesturing toward the rings.

"We'll see," answered Costance. "If you do, I'll be waiting." All feeling of kinship with the man drained from Orfin's heart.

9

Planning for the great society was much easier after the introduction of the first Ceretrak 500. Mirabella Quan and Blane Wallerton had managed to keep the addictive overtones out of the advertising and promotion of the devices. Instead, it was explained as a refreshing and powerful form of biofeedback. If people preferred it to all the other pleasures of life, well, they argued, that was not their design.

On the positive side, they argued, sexually transmitted diseases declined dramatically. Of course, the birth rate also dropped, much to the consternation of religious groups which denounced the devices as being "anti-family". This drawback was eliminated by the use of the *Discontinueds* as surrogate mothers. Not only did this bolster the birth rate among phasing couples, it also eliminated pregnancy as a possible barrier to the practice of cerebral stimulation.

In the end, legislation was adopted to assure that the Ceretrak was perceived as a technological underpinning for family values. Having developed from cell phone technology, the first prototype used an earpiece that supported tiny speakers. When it was learned that pressure points of the wrist provided even greater efficiency for delivering the effect, wrist units were quickly adapted. Matching wrist bands became the public emblem for married couples, replacing the custom of exchanging rings. While this new trend was largely symbolic, other refinements also promoted the perception of family values. The frequencies for phasing were shared by couples, but accessed by separate passwords. In this way, a successful phasing required shared timing and cooperation. Divorce or separation meant that rights to frequencies would be tied up in the judicial proceedings, and that neither party would be able to phase until the courts had been satisfied. The result all but closed domestic relations courtrooms. In surveys, couples registered high levels of satisfaction with their spouses, while failing to answer simple questions like, "What is your partner's favorite color?"

When the use of the device was banned from all correction facilities, the crime rate took a dramatic plunge. The same was true of illicit drug use. Of course, the use was rationed for the greatest good of society. It was a "perfect addiction" administered worldwide by the Quan/Wallerton Group. If there were rumors that the Planetary Council abused its power, well, that went with dirty politics anyway. The one thing they couldn't control was the name of the device. The flowing script that spelled out Ceretrak 500 never could compete with the generic street name that described it more accurately, *the Daytripper.*

If there was one imperfection with the plan, it was that some people seemed invulnerable to its benefits. Annually, the Council ran opinion polls and calculated that about eight percent of the general population would willingly sacrifice their own pleasure for grand ideals. What was more alarming was that an increasing minority was willing to suffer to see that those values were extended into the leadership of the planet. It was this statistical information that troubled Mirabella Quan and Blane Wallerton. Their positions on the Planetary Council were unchallenged, yet there was growing unrest among the general population regarding the restrictions on the use of the Ceretraks.

Many users were beginning to believe that their own access was too limited, while others enjoyed more liberal usage. To top it all off, several prominent attorneys were precipitating a class action suit in order to challenge the restricted use of the millifrequencies required to operate the devices.

The pact that had begun with a frenzy of sexual passion had begun to cool. Mirabella and Blane turned their attentions to other forms of recreation. The fact that they had unlimited access to the device meant that they had an unlimited number of volunteers to fuel their obsessions. They continued, however, to abstain from the use of the Ceretrak, while granting generous usage to those who were amenable to their suggestions. Rumor had it that their parties defined debauchery, but no one ever stepped forward to attest to the talk of sadomasochism and bestiality that became their entertainment. It was on one such occasion that the next phase of their plan took shape.

"The polls came out today," stated Blane.

"And were they as bad as we thought?" asked Mirabella, who was leaning over the balcony and staring into the inner courtyard below. A small crowd of onlookers had their eyes riveted on a couple centered on a small dais. The woman wore a black leather hood with nose, eye, and mouth openings, and a black leather corset. The man wore a hood with a drawstring pulled about his neck. Otherwise, he was entirely naked and bound to a chair. It was the victim and the executioner. She walked about the seated man examining his flesh, and periodically poking him with an electric prod. He would jump at the contact, and the crowd would wail their approval.

"Do they like that?" asked Blane.

"She does, I think, and he likes the increased access that a little pain can bring," observed Mirabella. "I think you can get anybody to do anything with that machine. Sometimes I wonder why we don't use it ourselves."

"Go ahead. Then I'll have the planet to myself," quipped Wallerton. "Actually, if you believe the polls, there are a number of people out there who could depose us if we don't keep on guard."

"The ones who can't be addicted?" asked Quan.

"Or at least they aren't satisfied with what the machine can do," offered Blane.

"What about a more potent machine? Could that be done?" said Quan.

"I don't know," answered Wallerton. "I was thinking that if they aren't controllable by the pleasure we offer, can we keep them distracted? After all, if they seem to suspend their own desire, they may show the same resistance even to higher doses."

"I see what you mean," said Mirabella, turning from the entertainment in the court below. "It sounds like you have something in mind."

"It's just an idea. Suppose, just suppose, that there was a virus that made people sterile, and it seemed to be genetically triggered."

"But I never heard of a gene that controls non-conformity," she challenged. "Could we get one engineered that would hit the right percent of the population? How could we control the spread? I mean, what if the law of chaos kicks in, and it hits us?" asked Mirabella in a concerned tone.

"That's the beauty of it," smiled Blane. "We don't actually need a virus, just the system to diagnose it!"

Quan brightened, then laughed out loud. "I love it! We have our medical teams diagnose the dissidents, and who knows? Maybe the virus will turn out to be fatal?"

"I knew you'd understand!" answered Wallerton. "But we don't want the bubonic plague; that would cause widespread panic. No, we just want enough cases to raise concern. Then we discover a genetic test, and effective medications to control the spread of the virus in those who are susceptible."

"And, let me guess, the medications affect mental function?" offered Mirabella.

"Or suppress libido, induce sterility, or all of the above," said Wallerton, in a tone that said he was proud of himself.

"And we could find funds to set up local support groups, and medical support for those for whom the virus could not be controlled. We'll be humanitarians," laughed Quan.

"Probably be made rulers of the world," added Blane.

"We already are that," grinned Mirabella, "We'll just be the unchallenged rulers! Who do we need to entice to pull together the lists of those who are infected with this virus-X?"

"*Virus-X*, cute, I like it, but I also have the perfect man in mind. He's a little twit with a sadistic streak and a large dose of megalomania," declared Wallerton.

"Let me guess. Is the twit a pudgy bore named Buford?" interjected Mirabella.

"That's the very man, Buford Costance! He'd kill for the chance to lick our shoes."

"Then let's give him the chance to do what he wants," said Mirabella. "We are, after all, in the pleasure business."

"Speaking of pleasure," noted Blane, "what do you say that we send the other members of the Council home, or offer them access to the Ceretraks?" He nodded toward the crowd below.

"What about our entertainers?" mewed Quan.

"How 'bout inviting them to a private performance?"

suggested Wallerton. "Have you ever made love to someone when *they* were on the Ceretrak? You can do anything; and they just keep loving it!"

Mirabella looked over the balcony. The man was somewhat slumped over; perhaps he had passed out. "You just want to unpeel the leather wrappings off the babydoll. You should know that she's a real 'screamer' on the Ceretrak. She's a show, all in herself."

"All the better," replied Wallerton, "what's her name?"

"She goes by *Vienna*, but she probably changes her name as often as she changes her hair color."

"Well, no matter, let's make them both scream," suggested Wallerton. "What do you say?"

"I'll tell the staff to get out the wrist rings for our guests."

10

Orfin didn't know exactly where he was headed when he left the Ambassador's quarters. The corridor went to the left and to the right, but he had been in this facility for less than twelve hours. In that short time, he had lost his partner and his trust in the representative of his planetary government. He wondered how anyone ever considered this place safe for Citizen

Explorers, when so little was known.

If he went to the right, he would be headed out toward a larger corridor that led to the ship and to the sunlit atrium. He turned to the left. Costance had said that the "Froggies" never came down this way because of the darkness. But if that were true, why was it made? Or were there other forms of life here that were yet unknown? Whatever he might find, for now, he preferred the path of darkness. He wanted to be swallowed by it, hid within it, and lost in the oblivion of his aloneness. He began to walk faster.

Beneath him the smooth hard floor began to slip away faster and faster. He could see nothing ahead, and if he had looked, nothing behind. He stretched out his arms to feel the sides of the dark corridor, but nothing met his touch. He began to zig and zag trying to feel anything, some point of reference. There was nothing. He could no longer see his hand in front of his face. He must be in a large open space. Aware that the floor seemed level, he began to realize that it could suddenly drop off into a crevasse, and that he would find himself hurled into oblivion. He ran faster. The only sound was his heart pounding in his head. He hurled himself at the darkness, and the darkness received him.

He stopped running. His side ached. His chest was heaving.

He cried out at the top of his lungs, and a thin voice met the air and fell flat. He dropped to the floor. It was cool against his sweating flesh, like a granite tombstone. Around him was the darkness, but he was not alone.

Something, someone was in the darkness. He held his breath to hear its breathing, but it held its breath, too. It was close, very close. He flailed his arms at it, but came away empty. Finally, he spoke, "Who are you?"

Something spoke. It was a thin voice. He thought it was his own, echoing off a distant wall. He thought it was his mother's voice, then Borthid's, then all the voices that ever uttered a kind word to him. It spoke his name, "Paul!"

Only Borthid knew that name. "Who are you?" he called out again. Then he remembered that was Borthid's question, and he remembered her answer later, "I know who you are!" He found himself saying it: "I know who you are!"

"Do you?" came the answer. Orfin's only refuge was silence. "Why are you throwing yourself away?" came a question.

"Am I?" asked Orfin.

"You race against the darkness, but you will not overcome it. Do you want to see Borthid?"

"Yes, yes," was his reply. "Is she alive?"

"She is safe. She is the one chosen. She is in the light." The assurances sounded like a puzzle. "Do you want to join her?"

"How do I find the way?" he cried in the darkness.

"Follow me!" was the swift reply.

"Where are you?" questioned Orfin.

"Beside you!"

"Which direction do I go?" he pleaded.

"Take a step," was the reply. "When you are at the center of the darkness, every direction leads you out."

Orfin began to walk. A moment earlier he had been running pell-mell without regard to direction or safety. Now each step was an uncertainty. There were no markers or directions to consult, no distant horizon to steer by. At each step he asked, "Is this the right direction?"

The voice answered, "You are doing fine; keep walking."

Hours seemed to pass, or else time had no meaning in that darkness. He was not sure of anything, not even the voice that he was compelled to trust. He took a sharp turn to the left, then two steps, and to the left again. He measured each step one, two, and then left again with two more steps. One more turn, to the left, one, two, and he stopped in his tracks.

"How am I doing?" he asked.

"You are doing fine; keep walking," came the answer.

"I can't be doing fine," he snapped back. I just walked a

square. I am in exactly the same spot I was eight steps ago."

"Are you?"

Orfin's certainty seemed less infallible at the calm challenge. He did not let on. "Of course I am! Even in this darkness I know that I have doubled back on my course!" he chided. "What sort of guide are you?"

"I am the guide you have, the one that you have now tested, and I ask you why you think you are in the same place as before?"

Orfin let out a cynical grunt, "This is pointless! You are not leading me anywhere!"

"Of course I am not," said the voice calmly. "You are leading me, and I have chosen to be your companion. I am following your steps."

"You are following me? I don't know the way out. I am trusting you to find the way out of this darkness," shouted Orfin.

"But how would I know the way?" was the answer. "Is not this your darkness? You must lead the way out. I am just here so that you know you are not alone, Paul."

"Why do you call me that name? Who told you that I was *Paul*? Have you talked to Borthid? Is she alive?" His questions trailed off to emptiness. There were no words, no answers. Orfin felt a tear running down his cheek and a lump formed in his throat, a lump so thick he could not swallow. He took another step into the darkness.

"You are doing fine; keep walking." The voice was back.

Orfin's feet seemed heavy as he lifted one foot and set it down in front of the other. He thought about counting them and changing directions, or stopping altogether, but it seemed futile, and his companion was either unable or unwilling to help. "Why did you tell me that I was not in the same place, back there?" asked Orfin, who was surprised by his own asking. He was not sure that he wanted an answer or if he just wanted to hear a voice.

"You were at the same spot, but you were not there in the same time," was the softly spoken response.

"What? Is this a riddle? If I was in the same spot, then I was in the same place," Orfin's voice was returning to its impatient tone.

The voice continued to speak in its matter-of-fact tone. "Child of earth, you were not in the same place because the place has changed in time. It has drawn closer to its fulfillment."

Orfin extended his arms and swept around trying to touch the voice.

"You are reaching too far," said the voice. "I am too close for you to touch." Orfin suddenly realized that he was not sure whether he was actually hearing a voice through his ears or a voice within his brain, as if words were being placed at the center of his consciousness. But they were distinct words, distinct from his own shaping of them. Was this voice telepathic? He took another step.

"What is this darkness? Is it another portal?" he asked, hoping to keep the voice speaking.

"This darkness is the one you brought with you. It is a place in time, not in space. Whether it is a portal or not depends on the way that you find."

"Do you always talk in riddles?" Orfin protested.

"Why do you think this a riddle? I have spoken plainly, but you do not comprehend. What is not plain to you, may yet be plain even as it is spoken. You want me to guide your steps; yet, walking will not lead you out of this darkness. I have told you that the darkness is yours, and that it is in time, not in space. It will be cleared when you choose to see and not when you pass to another place."

"Why then do you tell me that every step I take is fine? Am I traveling in the right direction, or not?" Orfin pleaded.

"You do not have to take any steps to find a way out. It is the time you spend here that is significant. It is your longing to be in the light that is the hopeful step."

"Riddles! You just speak riddles!" shouted a frustrated Orfin. The darkness seemed to thicken.

"Sit down, Child," urged the voice with a gentleness that could not be resisted. "Sit still in the dark until you understand."

Orfin sat, squatting on the smooth cold floor. The chill went through him. He listened for sounds. There was nothing to hear. He tried to sense the movement of air, but there was none to feel. He strained every sense, and all came back empty. A flash of panic hit him. "Are you there?" he cried.

"Of course," came a calm reply.

He tried to follow the source of the voice, but there was none. Or the sound was everywhere, he could not understand which was true. He strained again to sense something, anything.

"Why can't I find you?"

A voice of infinite patience answered. "Why do you persist in looking only in space for that which is only in time, Paul?"

"Why do you call me Paul?" he queried.

"Is not that your name?"

"It was, but I changed it. That's not me anymore!" he answered.

"Is it so easy to change yourself? Did not your mother call you that when she held you in her arms? Did you not long for that name to come from her lips when breath had gone from her?"

"But it is the name of the man who left her alone!" he croaked from a throat nearly swollen shut with emotion.

"Did your mother hate him?"

Orfin had never considered the question. "I don't know," he finally confessed.

"Would she name her child for someone she hated? Or did she hate you, too?" The questions were beyond his scope.

"She loved me!"

"She loved Paul," corrected the voice.

"But I am Paul!" the words echoed in Orfin's head as he heard himself speak. "I am Paul, I am the one who was held, and I am the one who is alone!"

"Are you?" challenged the voice.

"I am alone! Borthid was the last, and she left, too! I am alone, can't you see that?" There was silence. "Can't you see that?" Orfin shouted louder. His words echoed from some distant surface and crumbled into nothing. Silence.

"I am alone!" Orfin called. His heart began to pound in his chest. He rose to his feet. He started to run. His pace quickened. His arms and legs pumped furiously as he ran, his side ached, his lungs burned raw, and the darkness did not end. At last, his churning feet betrayed him. He hit the floor hard, and slid on through the dark tomb. When his body and head stopped spinning, he gasped, "I am alone." His powdery tongue stuck to the roof of his mouth, and he spoke again, "I am alone, do you hear me?" The stagnant silence choked him. "O God, I am always alone!" His sweat froze to his skin as he pulled himself into a fetal position. He hugged his knees and waited. He would wait for the darkness to clear. He put a hand over his eyes to feel if his lids were open. He could not trust his senses. "Damn you! Damn you!" he cried. His own voice sounded like a stranger's. Spent of all emotion, he whispered to the blackness, "Are you still there?"

"Of course, Paul," came a calm, quiet reply.

"What do you need from me?" he asked.

"Nothing."

"Then, what do you want from me?" demanded Orfin.

"Only that you would know your own name, and not be ashamed to speak it."

"My name is Orf..." he stopped the word in mid-syllable. He spoke again. This time his voice was a nearly muted whisper, "My name is Paul, and I am not alone." Then he added, "I suppose I never was."

Something changed, but in the static darkness, Paul could not name it. Then what filled his senses hit his consciousness.

There was a breeze, a cool breeze, like wind over the water, and with it came the dawn.

He was on a planet that had two suns, and knew no darkness, yet he was seeing a darkness lift like a fog rising. For the first time, he could see his surroundings. He had thought himself in a cavern or wide maze of twists and turns. But he was in the open. He was seated on a plateau of perfectly smooth white stone. He could see the horizon stretching ahead of him. He spun on his knees looking for the portal or entrance that had led him to this spot, but the horizon line circled him. The swirling darkness was about six feet off the ground now, though it was hardly a darkness. It was like a seething cloud, beautiful in its turbulence, catching the stray light rays and casting tiny spectral shapes all around Paul.

There was no one close by, and Paul wondered who had been speaking. In the far distance, however, a shape was moving. Paul studied the emerging form. It looked like one of the Photosynthoids, except that its shuffling gait was replaced by long, smooth strides that carried it quickly. It also seemed larger than all the others because it could be seen from a great distance. Paul was not frightened and, as if on cue, he rose to his feet and began walking toward it. His pace quickened until he was no more than twenty yards from the creature. Both stopped and stared. The being was magnificent in splendor, and Paul could not help but think that this must be a different species than the servile Froggies of Costance's world.

What he had mistakenly thought was larger size and greater bulk was actually a large hood of verdant skin that rose from the back of the creature to form a canopy. Actually, the Photosynthoids that he had seen before were exactly the same, but the flap of skin was folded and gave the impression of a hunched back. This had only added to their fawning and comedic appearance.

"Are you the one who was here in the darkness with me?" asked Paul, finding his voice.

"No," came a strong resonant word, "I did not enter the darkness, but I have come to you now in the light."

"Then who was talking to me?" said Paul, with a confused tone.

"The Shadduah would know," came the answer. "Perhaps it was even the Shadduah who spoke. This is a listening place."

"Is the voice, then, a power that lives in darkness?" asked Paul.

"The Shadduah holds the darkness," was the mysterious reply. Paul would have asked for an explanation, but it was spoken as though the meaning was obvious and he should already understand. Before he could make a reply, however, the Photosynthoid turned and began to stride away. Though the creature was moving at what seemed to be a comfortable pace, Paul was forced to run to keep up. He could not see where he was headed because his line of sight was obstructed by the green canopy of the Photosynthoid's back flap. Suddenly the creature stopped and with a flutter of sinews like the hood of a giant green-frilled lizard, the Photosynthoid folded its canopy. Its diminished proportions brought back the images of the first Photosynthoids that Paul remembered seeing when he left his ship. The new line of sight brought an image that Paul had never expected. He was on a flat crystalline plateau that stretched endlessly behind him, but before him was a precipice so sheer and deep that it dwarfed any earthly proportions.

"I have brought you here, as you have requested," spoke the Photosynthoid.

"I asked to come here?" puzzled Paul. He scanned the horizon. Below him was an endless valley of white sands.

"This is the *high place*. The place the Chosen One requested to come," was his cryptic answer.

"You mean Borthid?" corrected Paul. "Did she come through the darkness, too? Where is she now?" he asked.

"You have many questions, and many answers must be

spoken before you can join her. This is where the Chosen One came. Here she heard the Voice of the Shadduah. But now she is in the place of healing."

"Healing?" said Paul with alarm. "Was she hurt? Did something happen to her in the darkness?"

"She did not come here through darkness. It was not with her," spoke the alien with a voice of patience. "Neither was she wounded. She comes for the healing of things long past."

"Where is the place of healing, how can I get there?" questioned Paul.

"It is across this valley," said the Photosynthoid gesturing to the expanse beyond the rim of the plateau. "It is a journey that you will have to make one day, but I do not think you are ready yet. If you wish, I will take you to her."

"Yes," said Paul without hesitation. The alien turned toward him, and in one powerful motion swept Paul into its arms. Paul struggled, but the grip that cradled him was too strong.

"Do not be afraid, Earthman," said the strange being. Paul looked up at the green face, and behind its head arose a canopy of green, veined with oranges and reds that looked like hues of different pigments. He felt a surging down draft. It took a moment for his mind to unravel the meaning of the sensation. They were in flight. Behind him the plateau fell away, and the valley below deepened.

11

Dr. David Jahren was a trained scientist endowed with keen skills of observation. Those skills served him as he stood before the members of the Planetary Council. In the first ten minutes of his presentation, he realized that he was really speaking to two people. Though he was not politically astute, he could see in the body language and eye contact of the audience that only two people seemed to be actively considering the impact of his discovery. Those two were the leaders of the opposing parties, Mirabella Quan and Blane Wallerton. His news of the discovery of a new planet was revolutionary, and he knew it. His fear was that the politicians would miss a tremendous opportunity for the advancement of scientific exploration.

He had come prepared with charts and documents, formulas and plotted courses. He was to explain how to meet the challenge of traveling to a new oxygen-rich galactic way-station. Like many scientists, he had an affinity for data. His fear, however, was losing his case. It would not be for lack of facts, but under the realities of world politics, which seemed immune from scientific logic. It was clear that he was losing his audience.

By the end of his allotted time, he found it difficult to raise his head out of his notes. His concluding remarks were cut short by a council page who appeared to announce that the assembly's work schedule had been so grueling that they each had been allotted an additional phasing. The room cleared quickly, leaving Dr. Jahren and two others, the two most powerful leaders on the planet.

"Dr. Jahren?" asked Mirabella Quan. "Your work is very interesting. I hope you will excuse our colleagues, and consider our little threesome as a meeting of the executive committee, and not a sign of lack of interest on the part of the Council."

Jahren was confused, but accepted the comment as a spark of hope, after such a dismal beginning. "Thank you," he said, "I was afraid that I was not making my point with the others. This is a very important find. It is the missing element in deep space travel."

"We couldn't agree with you more, Dr. Jahren," added Wallerton. "The thing that we are concerned with is how to elevate such a discovery without its getting lost in the miasma of politics."

"That's exactly what I feared, too!" reacted Jahren with renewed enthusiasm. "I'm not sure what the others understood, but this is the second half of the puzzle of intergalactic space travel!"

"Can you refresh our minds about that?" asked Quan.

"Well," began Jahren, "we know that that we can surpass light speed. Yolandro proved Einstein wrong on that count, and she was able to demonstrate it. The drawback has always been the requirements on the ships that can achieve such velocity."

"I remember that now," interrupted Quan, "the ships cannot have any metal parts or contents."

"It's kind of like throwing a cosmic fastball," continued the Doctor. "If it's on target, there's no problem. Throwing a ship 150 light years with no margin of error is, or was, a major obstacle. Until now!"

"Wait a minute, I guess I'm not following you," stated Wallerton with a puzzled expression. "I thought that this new planetary discovery just gave us a place to go?"

Jahren's excitement was growing, "No, much more than that! Because this place has a rich atmosphere, we can harvest gasses at that end to renew compressed air thrusters that keep the 'pitch' on target. This place could be a sort of refueling station for even farther excursions!"

"But getting back is a problem?" queried Blane Wallerton.

"Yes, the travelers would have to leave earth forever. That's the other 'plus' to this discovery. We, at least, can give them a homeland at the other end, rather than dooming them to a cramped cabin with no hope of a life at all," Jahren's words trailed off. "In theory, we could have sent humans out a decade ago, but no one would want to doom them to never standing on land again. With this information, there are those who would volunteer for such an adventure. There are still pioneers out there, you know, free thinkers."

"We know," agreed Quan. "They are our best citizens. Please, understand, Dr. Jahren, that all this is overwhelming. Would you mind if Blane, err, Mr. Wallerton and I continued in private conference while you waited outside? In fact, we just got word that the Ceretraks have completely repowered. We'd be glad to provide you with a wrist ring to make your wait more comfortable."

"No thank you, Ms. Quan," answered Jahren. "I know you mean well, but I am personally opposed to those devices. In fact, I don't even possess one." Quan and Wallerton looked at each other.

"How did you manage that?" asked a startled Quan.

"Oh, just a little Space Agency sleight of hand," Jahren answered with a childish grin. "It's amazing what changing a digit in a data record will do. Some citizen out there gets double phasings every day and obviously hasn't been complaining. It sure saves me a lot of trouble. I really do not mind waiting."

"Very good," said Blane Wallerton. "Your work is very impressive, Dr. Jahren. We'll send a page to escort you to a more comfortable waiting area." He and Mirabella Quan left the room in silence.

Once outside, Quan turned to Wallerton and said, "What do you think?"

"I think we're playing with dynamite, and we need to go to a quiet room. This could be the answer to more than the space agency's wanderlust." By now, they were standing outside a door marked *QR-4*, the fourth floor "quiet room". Wallerton slipped an identity card in the bar code reader, the door opened, and the electronic masking devices engaged. Wallerton went to a console in the corner of the room, entered his identity code, and typed a message:

> Dr. David Jahren is waiting in the fourth floor presentation room. Escort him to holding area 4-A and see that he is comfortable. He is not to leave this area until further instructions have been given by me or Representative Quan.

Wallerton shut down the com station. "This would be a whole lot easier if we had voice recognition," he observed.

"Yes," remarked Quan, "but it would also make it easier to

bypass the security of the quiet room."

"And we're the only two who have that privilege," added Blane as he slid his arm around her. She backed away.

"It is amazing what you can do with a very little machine that knows how to make the brain play," retorted Quan. "Which brings us to the subject of one Dr. David Jahren, who seems to have a natural immunity to what we have to offer."

"I think we will need to decide about him before he leaves the building, but we have to make sure that we have enough information," warned Wallerton. "What do you think are the implications of this discovery?"

"I think the timing is perfect. We know that the *Discontinueds* are restless. Couldn't we send them off on a one way trip?" asked Mirabella.

"That was my idea, too," added Blane. "We convince them that a new colony can be established and that travel between the colony and earth will become as regular as e-mail. Then we line up the volunteers to begin a new world. It looks as though there will even be a way to recycle the ships."

"Maybe we don't want volunteers, so much as lottery winners," said Quan. "Think of it this way. We've tried to divert their rebellious tendencies with the introduction of the virus," she grinned at Blane, "and we could now hold out a completely random chance for a real adventure. We'd have them glued to the screen every night for a public drawing. We could even have reports of daily life on the other side and make them insist that we increase the flow of travel."

"And," commented Blane, "we could easily choose the winners from among the most restless, now that Costance has set up the database of psychological profiles to those on his virus list."

"That fellow is beginning to worry me," noted Mirabella. "He's too thorough. I'd bet anything he's also got a file on us that would turn up if something were to happen to him."

"I've had the same thought," agreed Wallerton. "But maybe Jahren's little 'way-station' can solve that problem, too."

"What do you mean?" queried Mirabella.

"Only this, we don't need Dr. David Jahren's discovery to start transporting the *Discontinueds*. We could have been shipping them out with no destination at the other end. After all, we did discover a non-existent virus. Wouldn't a non-existent planet be just as easy?" Quan raised an eyebrow. "Jahren has done us a favor. He's given us a real place to which we can issue one-way passes, but, because it's real, we can place an agent there who will return our ships to be used again."

"So we make Costance our agent," stated Quan, who began to

see Wallerton's plan.

"Nothing so lowly as that," sneered Blane, "Not for someone as significant as Buford Costance! I think he should be the Ambassador or Planetary Governor. What do you think?"

"I think it's perfect! Knowing that creep, he'll probably see it as a stepping stone to get back here for our jobs," said Quan sarcastically.

"But he'll never get back," offered Blane. The two laughed until tears ran down their faces. Regaining his composure, Wallerton walked across the room and reactivated the com station. He smoothly entered a code that threw an image on the security screen from holding area 4-A. The downward video angle showed a patient David Jahren lost in a scientific journal. "Ah, good Doctor," he muttered, "too bad you don't take advantage of the pleasures that we can offer you."

"Speaking of pleasures," added Quan, who began to tear open the fasteners of her Council uniform. "Let me see if this little power trip has done to you what it's done for me."

Wallerton twisted his torso so that she could see the growing bulge that distended his uniform. "Patience, Spider Lady," he chided, "I have one more detail to attend to." He typed an order on the console:

> When the phasing is complete, Buford Costance
> is to report to QR-4 for a top security conference
> with Representatives Quan and Wallerton.

"Now," said Blane, looking at his watch, "he won't be here for at least twenty minutes. I'm at your service, Bitch!"

12

Buford Costance wasn't really surprised when the security guards approached him at the conclusion of the Council's additional phasing. He had been the one who initiated the order on a signal from Quan. He did not know what sort of presentation Dr. Jahren had given, but the coded electronic message that came over his pager was emphatic. He was to get the room cleared by using the emergency codes that Wallerton and Quan had entrusted to him.

He trembled when he read the message because it also had additional meaning for him. Special phasings were always rewarded to him whenever granted to the Planetary Council. He had been waiting for one of those rare occasions to offer it to an *Alpha* named Vienna. She was the most magnificent woman he had ever seen, tall and slender with narrow hips and a taut body that men would die for. Rumor had it that some had, but he attributed that to the fact that Vienna's perfection had become her trap. Wallerton and Quan used her as entertainment in the private gatherings of the politically elite. Costance hated them for that, but he also needed them, and he needed Vienna. He could not hope to lure her to himself without being able to supply her addiction, and so far, that was beyond him. Addiction was the domain of the Quan/Wallerton Group, and they were not ready to take on another partner.

He did, however, have some privileges beyond those of mere mortals. He had access to surveillance information, and the codes that gave him entry to every database on the planet. He had a database of his own, too, the record of the private assignments ordered by Wallerton and Quan. He did not trust his private information to electronic media. He knew too well that any system could be breached, and so he relied on his own low-tech record and the hope that his hidden records would be his salvation, or at least a sympathetic epitaph. The system he used was a simple binary code, but it was camouflaged as a collection of antique playing cards. He spent hours arranging the individual decks according to a sequence of red and black cards in groups of eight. He then placed the decks in sequence. It took nearly twenty-three of decks to compile a simple message:

> There is no virus. I compiled a list of dissidents
> who are being drugged to exhibit symptoms.
> This was ordered by Mirabella Quan and Blane
> Wallerton.

With another eighty-two decks, he listed strands of data within the government databases that could be linked to make a *prima facie* case to corroborate his accusations. At first, his plan had given him peace of mind, but as he worked on Quan and Wallerton's covert activities, he began to realize that every level and department of government was controlled by those who watched the clock and measured time by the phasings of the Ceretraks. One by one, he found that those who did not live for the machine were turning up on his lists of those to be told that they had been infected by a potentially fatal virus.

Costance wondered where the data was coming from. These were not people who belonged to subversive groups or signed petitions of protest. They were leaders with a stake in the planet, and with a sense of service to humanity. It was quite by accident that he discovered the link, the answer as to how Quan and Wallerton were able to identify those people who were immune to their "favors" as they preferred to call them. The breakthrough came while he was in the office of a computer technician who was trying to show him a potential new access sequence to protect planetary government files. Computers were not Costance's forte, but someone or some group had gained access to level 15 security files. Representatives Quan and Wallerton called him in, and immediately ordered tracers on all log-ins. Whoever the perpetrators were, however, they always seemed to be one step ahead and never approached the access in the same way. Costance was placed in charge of new access codes that would render all the old ones useless. To his distress, competent help was not readily available from among the government's cyber-cryptographers. Most seemed incapable of original thought, and each new generation of codes was a predictable evolution from the one preceding it. Predictability in the world of cyber-cryptography is a terminal illness, or at least that was how the joke went. Nevertheless, each new code was rewarded by extended use of the Ceretrak, and predictable codes could be mass produced at a quicker rate than effective ones.

Jennifer Bertram seemed to be the exception to this trend. She was the stereotypical egghead type, or at least that was how Buford Costance saw her. She was a relatively low-level employee since she did not seem as "productive" as other members of the department. Costance found her to be an original thinker, a mathematician who was also an artist, and the combination made the freckle-faced, bespectacled woman a marvel.

The two spent hours together, and Buford's admiration for her grew. One day as they were working in her paper-strewn cubicle, he noticed a fully charged wrist ring sitting on a storage cabinet.

"It looks like you're entitled to a break," he said.

"That thing is more trouble than it's worth," answered Jennifer. "Take it if you want it."

"You *are* kidding, aren't you?" was Costance's reply. "People would kill for that," he added.

"Most people need to get a life," she countered. "I used to feel obligated about using the thing, but then I'd get involved in an interesting project, and then that thing would start yelling at me."

"What are you talking about?" queried Buford.

"It starts beeping! Haven't you ever noticed? I mean, if you don't use it within fifteen minutes, it goes off like an alarm. It used to drive me crazy. Once I went out to the coffee lounge to see if anyone wanted a phasing with it, and it was a free-for-all. Then for days afterward, people would bug me about using it next time, even people from other departments. It just wasn't worth it."

"So now you just use it yourself?"

"No, now it sits there, and yells at me a couple of times a day," stated Bertram, "but it's catching on. "

"It's catching on?" remarked Costance. "You lost me there! What do you mean?"

"It's really very interesting. I've never seen a spec sheet on those things, but I think I've got them figured out. It's a very interesting communication device."

"Communication device?" said Costance, with surprise in his voice.

"Yes, it is a sort of communication device. That's in addition to its advertised functions," Jennifer added with a smile. She turned to face Costance. He could see the wheels turning in her complex brain as though remembering the twists and turns of a maze. "The signal to begin a phasing is sent out from somewhere. Anyway, if fifteen minutes goes by and the wrist ring is not used, the charge sets off an audible signal to alert the owner. The first time it is ignored it sounds for about a half an hour in short beeps. Then it emits a long tone, sends out a radio signal, and powers down."

"A radio signal?" asked Costance.

"Yes, it's a primitive microwave signal. I figured that out by the interference it caused on my computer screen. After that, I was interested, so I began to observe it more closely. In fact, I kept a log on the thing. It's here somewhere." She shuffled through a file bin and retrieved a disk that she popped into her electronic book reader. "Look," she said, passing the pad to Buford.

He looked at the entries on the pad in his hand. In neat columns, Jennifer had noted the time of day, the length of time between repowerings, the duration and sequence of the alarm signals, and the time at which her computer monitor revealed radio interference. The pattern was obvious. The length of time between phasings increased and the alarm duration decreased consistently through the period.

"What do you conclude from this?" asked Costance.

"I figure that it's a built-in market survey," answered Jennifer. "Every user and their frequency of use is noted in a large database. What they've learned about me is that I don't use the thing, and they have virtually reduced my service to nothing, which is exactly what I want. It is very smart on their part. It's a slick operation. I don't like their product, but I sure can admire their efficiency."

Buford Costance weighed her words carefully. "Maybe politics has made me wary, but I would think that the information may be more than market research. You would be advised to use the thing every once in a while.... or give it to someone who would."

"Buford, you have to learn to trust more," said Jennifer with a twinkle in her eyes.

"Maybe," he answered, "but not all clever people are benign spirits."

*   *   *

As Costance approached the fourth floor quiet room, he knew he would soon be in the presence of two people who were not benign spirits. For a brief moment he puzzled as to why thoughts of Jennifer Bertram would flood his mind when summoned by Quan and Wallerton. His stomach muscles tightened as his fingers entered a code to tell the room's occupants that he was outside in the corridor. He waited. A cold sweat broke out all over his body. He dabbed his forehead with his sleeve, hoping to hide his tension when the door opened. When it did open, it was Mirabella Quan's imperious smile that greeted him.

"Buford, my friend, come in," she offered.

Her familiar tone seemed so disingenuous to Buford that it pulled him out of his fear and replaced it with an equally chilling manner of indifference. "You sent for me?" he spoke without inflection.

"Yes," countered Quan, dropping her affectations. "We have learned some things this morning which are going to change the world as we know it. At least, it will threaten the political balance if we aren't careful to take steps to assure that events do not get out of control. You are an astute observer, and know that the other members of the Council will never grasp the essential issues for maintaining stability during a time of rapid change, so Representative Wallerton and I have concluded that we need a partner. Your name was first in both of our minds."

Costance stepped back with a surprise that was visible to the two Council members.

"Maybe you should sit down, Buford," offered Wallerton. "In fact, we should all sit. If what we purpose is to be successful, we will all be working very closely together," he added with a sideways glance to Quan.

"Excuse me, if I seem to be taken off guard," countered Costance, "but I have no idea what you are taking about."

"And there's no reason why you should," answered Quan. "This morning a Dr. David Jahren addressed the Council about the discovery of a new planet. He and his colleagues are absolutely convinced that it will support human life, and that it can be reached in a relatively short time. I think he said nine months. Is that correct, Blane?" she asked, turning to Wallerton.

"Yes, nine months. He also believes that the resources of this planet will be adequate to refuel an air-jet propulsion system that will make even deeper space flights possible," he added.

"But I do not understand how this creates a potential instability?" said Costance. "The space agency can surely handle the technology, and the Council controls the agency's actions and budget. Where is the danger?"

"That's just it," continued Quan. "The technology is not so difficult that it couldn't be mastered by some group on the lunatic fringe. By preempting our actions, the people who oppose us could achieve a military staging area from which our whole civilization could be assaulted."

"But there's no evidence of any mass movement toward rebellion. Oh sure, there have been a few isolated cases of disgruntled citizens disrupting services and generally causing chaos, but it's very localized and short-lived. There seems to be no clear leader to rally the disenchanted," offered Costance in protest.

"None until now," interrupted Wallerton.

"Who?" asked Costance.

"We suspect that the man who discovered the planet has the potential of becoming the Father of a Revolution," stated Quan coolly.

"Jahren?" Costance was skeptical. "He's highly respected in the scientific community. What makes you think he would betray the system that he's spent his whole life serving?"

"There are several concrete indicators," answered Wallerton, "and, I'll admit, some speculation. Before we came into this room, he was confessing his fear that the politics of this discovery could hold back its usefulness in deep space exploration."

"So, that's an obvious complication. It is hardly evidence," protested Costance.

"Please, Buford," said Quan, "we are not presenting evidence so much as a profile. Jahren is an idealist. If he cannot further his work through the Planetary Council, he will turn to others who will be anxious to use his information. Trust me on this one. He has no qualms about this. What would you say if I told you that he's freely admitted modifying our government database?"

"Of course, he would," said Costance tiring of the innuendo game, "he has high level clearances. His experimental data would be entered into the database and he'd be expected to make changes and updates!"

"That's not what we're talking about," stated Wallerton with growing irritation in his voice. "He doesn't even possess a wrist ring and his name has not come up on your virus list. Why? I'll tell you why, because he's modified his wrist ring serial number so that his millifrequencies are being credited to someone else. You check his record. It will probably show you that he's never missed a phasing, and he doesn't even have a wrist ring anymore.... if one was ever even issued. He's cracked the level 15 codes. Does that set off any alarms for you?"

Costance's mind was swirling. He was working on the level 15 security breach, but his first thoughts were of Jennifer Bertram's discovery. She had unwittingly discovered the source of the names for his virus lists.

"Have you followed anything we've said?" pleaded Quan.

"Yes," said Costance, trying to snap his mind out of a sudden panic. "I understand why you are concerned. What do you want me to do?" It took every ounce of nerve to keep his legs from bolting. He needed to warn Jennifer. The wrist rings were everything that she had guessed. They were communicators, they were market research devices, and they were deadly dangerous to ignore. He tried to organize his thoughts. Mentally he steadied his voice to speak: "What should I do about this Jahren?"

"We knew you would understand, Buford," said Quan in her

patronizing style. "Dr. Jahren has become a danger to the order, though his sacrifice will be a loss to the space agency. When his accidental death is reported, I think it would be important to cut off all access to data files that originated from him or his research team."

"I understand exactly," said Costance, "but how am I to keep from thinking that one day I will be a danger to the *order*, as you call it?"

"That will not happen," replied Wallerton, "quite the opposite, in fact. This new planetary discovery must be handled correctly. The last thing we want is for citizens to cross out of the solar system with visions of establishing an alternate council. What we need to guarantee is that when they disembark their craft, they are met by an officer of our choosing. You, Buford Costance, are our choice to head a new planetary government."

Costance was caught off guard, but his quick mind turned to grasp the implications. "Would I be able to choose my companions?" he asked.

"Of course," assured Mirabella. "That would be our ambassador's privilege."

Immediately, Costance thought of Jennifer Bertram, but he dared not mention her name. Instead he was surprised to hear his own voice saying, "How about Vienna?"

"Vienna?" replied Quan, who gave a quick glance at Wallerton.

"Yes, Vienna," repeated Costance. In a flash he realized that he needed her addiction. He needed her unquestioned loyalty to the wrist rings.

"Yes, of course," said Wallerton, "it's a good selection for an extended diplomatic mission. She makes quite a diversion. Congratulations, Ambassador Costance, on the selection of the first member of your team." He extended his hand, and instinctively Costance accepted the gesture. "Dr. Jahren is in the fourth floor holding area; I trust we can leave him safely to your care?"

Buford Costance's mind stumbled over Wallerton's choice of words. He reflected for a moment, then nodded his agreement. "You will be safe with Jahren in my care," he said picking up on the ironic use of the word *safe*.

Mirabella had worked her way to the control console. The exterior door opened catching Costance in mid thought. The meeting was over.

"We will have more to talk about very soon," said Mirabella almost as an aside. The door closed behind him.

Costance looked down the long sterile steel corridor. No one was in sight as he fell back against the cold wall. His heart was racing. He had never been faced with anything of this scope. In a moment he would greet a total stranger with a handshake, and then improvise a way to kill him cleanly and outright. Quan and Wallerton wanted his help, but how could he deal with such people? His thoughts returned to Jennifer Bertram, and the wrist ring that sat in her cubicle. If he was to be the death of David Jahren, what he had just learned would be Jennifer's salvation. A life for a life was the best rationalization that his mind could fabricate. He found himself running down the passageway. He passed two intersecting hallways before reaching a public com-station. Panting, he entered his access code and the communications menu came on-screen. He typed in the address, jbrtrm6@ccrc.com, and entered his message:

> Jenny, I need to talk with you about the code sequences, but everything is crazy today. I haven't even had time for a break. Hey, why don't you use that wrist ring in my honor! (Please, as a friend, humor me!) See you soon, Buford.

He read the note again to see if there was anything an electronic censor could build upon or suspect. Seeing nothing, he entered the keystrokes to send the file. Now he would have to face Dr. David Jahren. "Don't think about it," he said to himself as he started down the corridor.

13

Paul was remarkably calm for a man suspended a thousand meters off the ground and in the clutches of a green-winged humanoid. For some unknown reason, fear seemed inappropriate as his eyes scanned the ground below. A moving black dot followed a path parallel to theirs, and he was tempted to shout over the rush of the wind to ask what it might be. Before he could form the words, he realized that it was their own shadow.

"What is below us?" he asked finally. His voice dropped off quickly in the turbulent air. He was not sure his companion had heard.

"That is the dwelling place of the Skree," came a clear answer. Paul began to suspect that the words he was hearing were not forced to his ears across the wind, but planted directly in his mind by some sort of telepathy.

"Who are the Skree?" he asked.

"They are the sharers," came the answer. "The Shadduah also holds the Skree."

Paul felt like he was still being spoken to in riddles. He

remembered the voice in the darkness saying, "What is not plain to you, may yet be plain even as it is spoken." This was one of those times. He could tell that the creature was speaking simple answers. Yet, in their simplicity, Paul had no context for understanding. If he was to learn, he would have to begin by asking questions with answers that would relate to his world of experience.

"Who are you?" he asked at last.

"I am myself," came the reply. Paul sighed.

"No, what is your name? What do you call yourself?" he said, his voice betraying a sense of frustration. Why was such a simple question so difficult to understand? Or was this creature playing with him? Was it withholding self-disclosure? And, why? "What do your friends call you?" he tried to create a context. He had no luck.

"I have no friends," was the cryptic answer.

Paul could sense his own frustration rising. "The others, what do they call you?"

"There are no others."

Paul stiffened. He had seen dozens of these creatures at the embarkation point and in the atrium. Why had he trusted this one? Where was he being carried?

"Don't be afraid, Paul," offered the creature. "I am taking

you to see your companion. Why are you surprised that there is only one of us?"

The creature seemed to be reading his thoughts and emotions all at the same time. Paul wanted to elude the creature in a daydream by retreating into the recesses of his own memory. He forced his mind to focus on a time and place long past, a picnic by a lake. He could smell a fish, a bluegill caught on a bamboo fishing pole. He felt the scales, and the spine of its dorsal fin pinching his soft hand.

"Your world is a beautiful place," said the Photosynthoid. The creature had followed him through the maze of his mental gymnastics.

"No!" shouted Paul, seeing his mother walking along the shore of the lake. The image was only a memory, but he did not want this stranger to see her. These were his thoughts, his memories. He did not want them invaded by an alien presence.

"We do not mean to frighten you, Paul, nor follow you into secret places. It is clear that we will not easily understand each other. In the Children there are no secret places, but we are confusing you."

Paul was confused, and the creature had sensed it. He went back to his simple questions. Perhaps one would be given an answer. "Why do you say that there is only one of you? I saw many of you before I came through the darkness."

"Now I understand," came the unexpected reply.

It had not occurred to Paul that the creature was as confused as he. "What do you understand?" he asked.

"That you are not connected. This is why you felt you had to go to her. We could not understand what you were feeling, and why you needed so desperately to be present with Miriam."

"Miriam?"

"The Chosen One has named herself, but you did not know that, did you?" observed the creature with the first shred of excitement that Paul had noticed.

"How could I have possibly known that?" stated Paul in an arrogant tone. "And, if there is only one of you, why did you just use the word 'we'?" he added angrily.

"Paul, set aside your anger. Try to understand things differently. The Children are one, though we are in many places. We are connected. When Miriam had named herself, I heard it and we knew it. These are your words that I am using. I do not understand the difference between 'I' and 'we'. Are they not the same?"

"If you heard it, then you must have been with her," stated Paul.

"Yes, and no. You do not yet comprehend. Be patient with

me; it is difficult for me to express this thought." Paul realized that his own frustration was matched by that of his companion. "We were there when Miriam named herself, so I knew it as she spoke the words. I heard it, but the part of us that is holding you now was not present with the Chosen One when she named herself. We are connected."

The words silenced Paul's confusion, and he remembered what the Ambassador had said at their aborted briefing. "If you correct their grammar," he had said, "they never make the mistake again, and it's all of them. It's like if you tell one, the others know it, too." This would explain it, Paul thought, but was it some form of collective consciousness, or merely that telepathic creatures could not help but overhear every thought on the planet? If that were the case, would their minds be full of noise?

"What is it like?" was the question that he finally asked when he broke the silence.

"I could ask the same question," was the reply. "We cannot imagine living with one voice, one perception, one breath. When you were in the darkness, I felt it though. I tried to speak to you, but you could not hear."

"Could you have been the voice that I heard then?" pleaded Paul.

"No, many of our voices spoke, but they were not the One who found you. We felt your aloneness. It was very deep, deeper than she who was Chosen, deeper than the Skree when they cry for aid."

Paul did not pretend to understand the answer, but he could not pass the reference to Borthid. "Can you tell me what has happened to Borthid?" he asked.

"She has journeyed far, and sings for joy. Her voice is like light for us. Perhaps it was the sound of her song that led the Shadduah to you in the darkness. That was the voice you heard, and except for that presence and the song of Miriam, I would have despaired for you."

A lump formed in Paul's throat. Through blurry eyes, he turned to scan the horizon. In the distance he could see that they were approaching another high plateau which marked the opposite boundary of the great sand rift. The sky was blue and clear, and light flooded the valley. He looked for the shadow of their flight, but it was gone.

"This is a time of no shadows," came an unexpected reply to an unvocalized question. "The second sun has risen, and we are surrounded in light. The Shadduah knows the light. The Shadduah pours it upon us."

To Paul, the words sounded like music, but he was not sure.

"What does it feel like? Being connected, I mean?" asked Paul.

An imponderable silence followed. It was accompanied only by the rhythmic beat of wings, and then the creature spoke with a voice so deep and broad that it might have been spoken by a unison choir. "We feel that we are ourself, and none other."

"How strange," thought Paul, "I fight to own my own name, and yet I do not know myself, and this one, who cannot or will not declare a name for himself, is at peace."

"Your names isolate you," offered the creature. "You use them to separate and to distinguish. We do have a name. We call ourself *the Children*. You could call us that."

"Thank you, Children," said Paul. It was very strange to use the plural word for a singular being, but it felt right. In fact, he thought, this alien world was beginning to feel more like home than any place he had known.

"Was that your mother by the lake?" asked the Children.

"Yes," said Paul, surprised by his own openness.

"We thought as much," came the reply. "We sensed your love when you saw her... and your sorrow."

"The two run together," answered Paul, sensing a wave of overwhelming exhaustion pouring over him.

"That is something we do not feel in our connectedness," said the Children. Paul didn't hear. Sleep had taken him.

14

When Paul opened his eyes, the brightness was overwhelming. He raised his right hand to shade his vision and realized that he was lying on his back facing upward. A shadow passed before his blinking eyes, and he realized that one of the Photosynthoids was standing in the path of the rays of the planet's blaring sun.

"Our places of healing are in the light," came the voice of the attendant, "perhaps it is not so well-suited to those whose eyes are weak."

"Am I in the place of healing?" he asked. "Is this the place where they brought Borthid?"

"Yes, and yes," was the reply. "She was here, and you will see her soon, but first you must gather your own strength." The creature leaned down to him and placed a cordial of *longstol* to his lips. "Drink this," he said.

Paul had not realized how disoriented he had become. The passage of time had none of the familiar markers of light and darkness. How many days had he been here? How many meals had he missed? He had no way of knowing except that as he sipped the *longstol* he realized that he was famished, and that each taste washed over him with a wave of contentment.

"Six days," said the Children, who had offered him the

beverage.

"What do you mean?" questioned Paul.

"You have been here for the passage of six of your earth days. This is your seventh day since you left your ship."

Paul was still not sure that he liked the creatures' apparent ability to discern his thoughts.

"Do not be afraid," said the Children. "Though your thoughts are open to us, we would not use them against you. That has puzzled us greatly. Why do you fear being known to yourselves?"

Paul felt the cobwebs clearing. "We all want to know ourselves; it just that we have learned to be careful as to whom we let in. The wrong person could abuse our trust. We have a saying, 'Knowledge is power.'"

"We have heard no such saying," came the answer. "We would not say that. We might say, 'knowledge is responsibility' or 'knowledge connects us.' Perhaps it is because we share all knowledge, it is more complete."

Paul was puzzled, but his fear of disclosure had subsided. "Why do you suppose I cannot read your thoughts?" he asked.

"That puzzles us, too," said the Children. "We are not hiding from you. Perhaps when you know that you have no power, the Shadduah will grant you knowledge."

With that, the lesson was over. Paul felt suddenly like a child waiting for the bell at recess. He wanted to blank-out his mind and run. It was not the temptation to run from anything, but to run for the pure joy of it. He had to ask one question. He felt himself delay, and then realized that there was no reason not to ask. The Children already knew his thoughts; they were merely waiting for his vocalization, to know if he was ready for the answer. "You know me," he said. "You know all my thoughts. Do you like me?"

He had not expected a long silence. The opinion of his hosts mattered to him, and he could not understand such a calculated hesitation. He began to fear his own question, and to distrust any answer so cautiously worded.

"It is not the answer that halts us," came the reply, "it is the question. We do not understand why we should like you or not, and why that should matter. You are Paul, you have life, you give life, and the Shadduah holds you. What could our liking or not liking add to that?"

It was not the answer Paul had expected, but it was an answer.

"Perhaps," continued the Children, "we shall learn from you and be able to know the answer to your question. That may yet come in time, but now," a webbed green mitt took Paul's hand, "now, you want to get up and walk." The creature was right. Paul rose to his feet, his shaky legs buckled as though he were a foal rising to greet the day for the first time.

Paul scanned his surroundings. It was another crystal dome of the same construction as the atrium near the Ambassador's quarters. This one was smaller, however, and the sunlit interior revealed alternating rows of raised divans and what appeared to be sand pits. On most all of the elevated platforms a Photosynthoid rested or was perched. Some were lying like sunbathers on a beach. Others sat erect with outstretched wings that were reminiscent of a great bird of prey drying its feathers in the morning light. The smell was familiar, and unmistakable; it was bread, or something much like it.

"What is this place?" asked Paul.

"This is the place of healing," came the answer as Paul walked the perimeter of the dome with one of the Children.

"Is everyone here sick, then?" he asked.

"No, not as you think," came the reply. "Here the strong and the weak meet to be reminded of their connection." Paul's confusion did not have a chance to settle down into a question before the answer was given. "The strongest of the Children come here to feed the weakest of the Skree, and the strongest of the Skree give breath back to the weakest of the Children. And when the breath of a Children stops, the Skree accept them back."

Paul realized that this explanation was supposed to make sense, but there were gaps in his knowledge. He knew that his confusion was heard, but he also knew that time and experience would awaken his understanding better than more information.

"You are becoming wise, Paul," observed the Children.

Paul smiled because he understood. "Maybe I am getting to be more patient," he added, "or more trusting." If silence can offer encouragement, it did so in that moment.

On the divan at the edge of the room, Paul saw another sort of figure. Whatever it was seemed out of place, and alien in that light. As he drew closer, Paul saw that it was another human, an ebony-skinned female. It was Borthid! She was lying motionless, barely breathing. He had never seen her like this, she seemed small and frail and she was naked. He ran to her, calling her name.

"She cannot hear you," said the Children. "You will not be able to awaken her."

15

As Buford Costance approached holding area 4-A, his mind

was weighing alternate possibilities. "Who was this Dr. David Jahren?" he wondered to himself. If he was the threat to the society that Quan and Wallerton had made him out to be, perhaps he was capable of being a strong ally. How would he know? Even if he could find reason to trust and confide in the scientist, he could not trust the walls of this building. He suspected that even the Quiet Rooms were not entirely safe. He needed a place, and it was not until he crossed the threshold of the room and saw the doctor that it dawned on him. A smile came to his face, and Jahren mistook it for friendliness.

"Dr. Jahren," he stated, extending a hand. "I am Buford Costance. Representatives Quan and Wallerton asked me to extend their apologies to you for not returning to talk to you. I serve as their attaché, and they have briefed me about your work." Costance attempted to size up Jahren as he played to the observation cameras that he knew had been activated.

"I've been thinking, Mr. Costance," urged the Doctor. "Is there anything else I can do or someone I should talk to about this discovery? It is of critical importance!"

"No," assured Costance. "You have impressed the right people. Don't confuse their absence as a lack of interest in your project. I have not seen them so excited in years. In fact, I am sure that at this moment they are working on ways to transform your ideas into practical reality."

Jahren relaxed his stance. Buford hesitated and then spoke, "Will you be headed back to your office over at CIPE?"

"Yes," answered Jahren. "My staff at the Center is waiting for my report. They are as anxious as I am. In fact, if I had access to a com station, I'd like to call them."

Costance thought for a moment. "No," he said hesitatingly. "I'm not sure, but I would think that this matter has to be handled with extreme confidentiality. An intercepted com message would make a field day for the press. I think it would be better to have our ducks in a row before too many details become widely known."

"I'm not very political," said Jahren. "I guess I just don't know how to think that way. At least that's what some of my team members say. They say that my coming to the Council is a waste of time, and that there are others who would listen."

Costance was tempted to blurt out what he was thinking, "Oh, shit!" he thought. "Why did you say that here, you fool!" But, the words that left his mouth were calm and civil. "Well, Doctor, you will just have to reassure them that the Council was receptive and will support every aspect of your work."

"That is a load off my mind," confessed Jahren.

"Might I suggest," offered Costance with a playful lilt in his voice, "that I give you your first lesson in covert behavior. Instead of your leaving by the door, can I offer you a diplomat's privilege?"

"What is that?" asked the scientist.

"I am going to trust you with some information that goes beyond even your security clearance," offered Costance. "Beneath this building there is a subway system that allows the sort of secret comings and goings that are sometimes required for sensitive diplomatic negotiations. In any case, you will be back at the Center for Interplanetary Exploration, and with your team, before the press knows that you've left the building."

Buford gestured for Jahren to follow. Before he could respond, Costance was leading him down the corridor in the opposite direction from the main entrance. The hallway was lined with larger than life portraits of the members of the Planetary Council. He stopped at a turbo lift and pressed the call button. "This is the door to the magic kingdom," chuckled Costance. The portal slid open. The two entered the unremarkable compartment, and the door glided closed. Costance simultaneously depressed the button for the third and fourth levels, and slid his identity card into what appeared to be the grillwork for an audio speaker near the emergency communicator.

"Good afternoon, Ambassador Costance," said a computer-generated voice as his identity card emerged from the reading device. The addition of the title, *Ambassador*, told him that Quan and Wallerton were well aware of his movements. Jahren had noticed.

"Ambassador?" he said. "Sounds like you've been promoted from attaché?"

"Yes," answered Costance. "But that's not for public consumption, not yet anyway. I told you that you were moving beyond your clearance level. Mum's the word!" The two smiled at each other when the door opened. Jahren was surprised because he had felt no sensation of motion.

"This is a special lift," stated Costance, anticipating Jahren's question. "I'll bet you'd be hard pressed to say that we even moved, much less to tell me a direction."

"You've got that right," answered an impressed Jahren. The two exited the lift.

"Straight ahead," instructed Costance, gesturing with his hand.

The diplomatic "back door" was not impressive. It was about five meters wide and cylindrical with smooth stainless steel sides. One side was cut away, but the darkness beyond made it look like a window on a black hole.

"Kind of like being in a sewer, isn't it?" suggested Costance. "It's built to be maintenance free, private, and with no corners in which to plant an explosive device. Those who bring an entourage use the front door."

"I guess so," observed Jahren as he stepped onto the platform. "I wouldn't think many could travel this route at one time."

"Six is the number," advised Costance. "The car has six places. When we entered the turbo lift my identity card authorized the dispatch of a transport car which should be along momentarily. It will take you to another stop like this one. A driver will be there to take you to the Center. No wrong turns are possible; there are no buttons to push or anything. I figure that with diplomats as the primary users, this thing had to be idiot proof." The two laughed. "Of course, I'll be with you to make sure that the driver is waiting for you."

Dr. David Jahren nodded his appreciation. In another time, the two could have been friends. Costance felt his ears pop as the pressure in the tube changed suddenly. A transport car was approaching at high speed, forcing air into the tunnel ahead of it. With a sudden powerful thrust Costance pushed the doctor into the black hole.

16

By the time Buford Costance returned to the turbo lift, sensors in the high-speed transport car had indicated to the dispatch center that some sort of collision had taken place. Such occurrences were not unique. No derailment or significant loss of speed usually meant that a vagrant or a stray dog had wandered into one of the connecting tubes that linked the Planetary Council Center to the public transport system. Because of its location, however, a maintenance team was dispatched and found the grizzly evidence.

Costance was in the fourth floor Quiet Room giving a more detailed report when word came that Dr. David Jahren's remains were found in a subway tube beneath the center. By that point all computer records showing that Costance had activated the turbo lift had been modified. The new data record revealed that Jahren had entered the lift alone, that he had successfully reached the boarding portal, but that a brief power failure took place as a transport car was passing the portal at high speed. The investigation would suggest that the momentary disorientation of the scientist had proved fatal when he stumbled into the path of the transport car.

"Good thinking, Costance," said a congratulatory Wallerton. "There have been rumors of the subway for years, and if the location of the least secure access port is discovered, there is no harm done. We might even get the press to report a different location for the accident as a part of their patriotic duty."

"And in lieu of losing phasing privileges," added Quan.

"This really isn't my line of work," said Costance. "Would it be alright if I slipped away for a while?"

"Of course, Buford," said Quan. "I think you've more than earned your ambassadorial appointment. But there is one more thing, a small assignment."

Costance cringed at the thought. Wallerton picked up on his change of expression. "Relax, Costance," said Blane. "It's a small thing. It'll be routine compared to what you've been through."

"Yes," continued Mirabella. "We're thinking about you, Buford. Security will be a critical part of maintaining the safety of your planetary outpost, and it is clear that once knowledge of this discovery gets out, even relative amateurs will be able to make their way there."

"Is the technology that simple?" questioned Costance.

"Apparently," responded Wallerton, "but because travel will be in engineless pods, travelers and their crafts will be vulnerable to earthbound shuttles." The look on Costance's face told the two Council members that further explanation was needed.

"Let me draw you a picture, Buford," said Quan with growing irritation. "The problem is here, right outside our atmosphere. The craft that could make this journey will be ceramic and plastic. Jahren made it quite clear that metals would cause havoc, even to the extent that people old enough to have fillings in their teeth would have to have their mouths reworked." The three laughed at the prospect.

"Nobody's that old," chided Costance, who was almost forgetting himself in the ridiculous nature of the statement.

"Exactly," continued Quan. "The fuel needed to achieve launch thrust will probably be carried in boosters which will be jettisoned before leaving our solar system. Only a small amount of gaseous fuel will be carried, and it will be exhausted at the landing at the other end."

"Great," sneered Costance, "half way across the universe and out of gas."

"Please, Buford, don't interupt," said Wallerton.

"Thank you, Blane," persisted Quan, her voice conveying her disapproval. "Spectral analysis has given us a good idea of the availability of gases in the atmosphere on the new planet. The fuel for the return will be harvested from the atmosphere by genetically altered bacteria. The technology is not difficult. Every indicator says that a vessel can not only launch successfully, but it can easily survive the return trip to our solar system. The problem is that it will arrive without reserve power. It would be incapable of negotiating an atmospheric reentry. The craft will just be adrift. Returning pods will be crippled. They will have to be collected by shuttles, and in that span of time, they would be sitting ducks for pirates."

"Wouldn't simple parachute technology work at this end?" argued Costance, who was beginning to follow the discussion. Quan looked at Wallerton as if pleading for help.

"It's too big a risk," said Wallerton. "There would be no margin for error. If the crew misguided the pod, they could burn up in our atmosphere or be deflected into the sun. We don't pretend to understand all this, Buford; we only know what Jahren reported. We know, however, that his data will support this."

"We also know that his team has contacts with others who could use this information," interrupted Quan. "We heard what he said to you in the holding area. The only way we can control this is to protect the production of the specialized craft, and to make sure that they do not become space salvage for those waiting in ambush for returning pods."

Costance found his mind swimming in the details. It had been an inconceivably complicated day. The talk of his being an ambassador had masked an obvious fact, namely that *he* would have to make a journey across space.

"I would think that you would have an interest in protecting the frontier," said Wallerton, trying to get the attention of a distracted Costance.

"Yes, of course," said Buford forcing himself back to the present.

"What we want you to do is develop a vehicle identification system, and find a way to get one installed in every craft capable of achieving even a low level orbit," instructed Wallerton. "But it must be done surreptitiously."

"What?" protested Costance.

"Really, Buford," said an exasperated Quan. Wallerton glared at her so that she held her anger.

"Listen, Friend, it's a small thing," continued Wallerton. "We can talk about it later, but here is the gist of it. We want you to develop a system so that we can pinpoint the location and identity of any craft that would approach the transport pods during their time of vulnerability. It could be some kind of beacon, or something that we could activate from a surface observatory. It has to be something that can't be disabled. From what Jahren said, we just can't be sure that anarchists or revolutionaries will not be waiting to harvest the returning craft with an eye toward establishing their own base of operation."

Costance seemed to understand Wallerton's last comment, but whether he would retain it was becoming questionable. Clearly, he was on the edge of exhaustion, and the two Council members realized that he was approaching his limit.

"Go home, Buford," they finally urged. Without much ceremony, Costance was alone in the sterile corridor.

17

From the balcony of his flat, Costance could watch the sun setting over the skyline of the city. He had never looked at the sky so carefully. He had led an earthbound life. His wisdom was based in a practical ethic of push and pull, until he could gain enough ground to call his own. His new assignment would be across the sky. That seemed beyond his influence, beyond his control.

Some had called him ambitious. He wondered what his mentors would think about their student on this day in his life. Today was the day when Buford Costance exchanged the resources of a quick mind and iron will with a simple push that ended the quick mind of Dr. David Jahren. His reward would be a world of his own, a place where he would be king, or at least regent. Today he had wagered the life of another, but the red-streaked sky reminded him that other lives were hanging in the balance. The gamble he was entering would place his own life in jeopardy. Soon, he would be sailing a galactic path to an unimaginable destiny.

What sort of world would he build for himself? It seemed an empty question. Ambition is a powerful ally, but no ambition would fill the emptiness of a barren planet. Even hours of phasings would not satisfy his deeper desire, to touch and be touched in the heart and mind. He closed his eyes and imagined the silence of an empty world. He wanted, he needed a companion. He wanted to have a place that knew both the comfort of silence and the flow of words. He longed for words that touched realities other than his own, and shared dreams that he had not yet dreamed. He was thinking of Jennifer Bertram.

Time passed, and glazed eyes saw the sparkle of steel and glass turn black against the retreating sunlight. The city lights emerged. Windows in other flats whispered of other lives and other hopes and terrors among the cliff dwellers of the urban canyons.

Costance took a deep breath and pulled himself to his feet. He was hungry. How long had it been since he had eaten? He could not remember, a lifetime at least. He slid open the door where warm, dry air washed over his mist-covered body. He shivered.

Across the room he saw his pride and joy, his famous collection of antique playing cards. There would be no room for them on a new world, at least not until parcels could be shipped, and needed supplies could be replaced by wanted possessions in cargo vessels. "These will have to be packed," he said to himself. After hearing his own voice, he realized that he had already made his decision. He would risk the sky to find a world of his own.

He opened a colorful box of cards and began to shuffle them. He opened a second box, and then a third. One by one, he shuffled the decks of his collection, until 105 decks lay stacked on the table in front of him. It was then that he noticed the blinking light on the com station. A message was waiting for him.

He walked across the room, entered his access code, and waited for the screen to burst to life. It was a computer generated memo:

> **Message Returned:** error code 08, no such addressee.
> To> "Jennifer Bertram" jbrtrm6@ccrc.com
> From>"BufordCostance"
> cstnc1@iph.gov.com

Jenny, I need to talk with you about the
code sequences, but everything is crazy today.
I haven't even had time for a break. Hey,
why don't you use that wrist ring in my
honor! (Please, as a friend, humor me!) See
you soon, Buford.

Buford stared at the screen. Five times he reread Jenny's e-
mail address. It was correct. There were no errors.

18

Paul was at a loss. More than anything he had wanted to find
Borthid, but this was an image more akin to viewing a corpse
laid out on a slab of translucent marble. The irony of the
Photosynthoid's words raced through his head. "She cannot
hear you. You will not be able to awaken her," they had said.

"Why can't I talk to her?" he cried out loud, rushing to her
side. He turned his head and pressed his right ear against her
chest cavity. Instinctively, he listened for a heart beat. It was
strong and regular. He sank to his knees.

"What is wrong with her?" he asked either with his voice or
to himself.

"She is well," said the Children. "She walks in the light, and
her singing feeds our hearts."

Paul was tired of riddles, and tired of the struggle to hold back places of his mind from his hosts; or were they his captors?

"How can you say, 'She walks in the light'?" he asked. "I can see that she is here and unconscious. Maybe Ambassador Costance was right. You are only interested in her carbon. Is she a carbonator for your hospital? You brought her here to enrich your healing place. Is that my fate, too? You want to keep us breathing, but not with any life we can call our own!"

"Stay with her, Paul," was the unexpected response. The creature backed away, retreating to another corner of the dome. The room was still. Paul looked for motion, but there was none. The Children appeared frozen like fantastic gargoyles or more properly like great jade-green chimaeras. In the silence, he heard only his own thoughts, and then the rhythmic breathing of the woman lying next to him.

He turned to Borthid. He did not know what he was seeing. Was she a lifeless form? Or, was he still such a child that he had yet to learn what life looked like? He began to weep as he shifted positions to sit beside Borthid's body. He pressed the palm of his hand against her warm cheek. Tears splashed against her ebony features.

Paul had no explanation for his crying, but it rose within him like a flood springing from years of rain. He wept until the sobbing came back as an echo that called him up short. As quickly and unexpectedly as it began, his mourning was ended.

As empty as the chamber had felt earlier, now it felt full. It felt pressurized, as though the spaces between everything were fuller and denser than the substance of reality, as though the dimensions of the invisible made everything thin and shadowy.

It was then that he heard it. It was clearly music, but his brain could not name it. There were words. He strained to catch them, as though they were a message to him. "You brought them in and set them on a high place," the song began. The melody was flowing with a haunting joy that made his sorrow cease. It seemed to come out of the walls and floor, maybe from the planet itself. Paul turned to look at Borthid. Her features were smooth and clear. She looked younger than he had ever seen her. She looked at peace, but most alarming of all, she was singing.

"Lie down next to her, Paul," said the Children who had silently returned to his side. Without questioning, Paul obeyed.

19

Paul's first impression was that something was stinging him. He opened his eyes to blinding sunlight, and a wind-swept sandscape. He was on the upper edge of a dune. The stinging was nothing more than sand carried on the wind battering his bare skin.

It was then that he realized that he was naked. Beside him was one of the Children in its diminutive form with folded wings. The Photosynthoid also seemed to be looking out across the dunes.

"Where am I?" asked Paul, not knowing how he should react to his own nudity.

"We thought you might like to walk in the sunlight. You are on the valley floor. The healing place is just there," they said, pointing to the top of an outcrop of crystal in back of them. "It was time for us to visit the Skree, and we thought you should learn about them."

"The Skree," said Paul. "Yes, I have wondered who they are."

"The Skree share life with us, the Shadduah holds the Skree," said the Photosynthoid as though reciting a creed.

"Where are they?" asked Paul. "Do they live far from here?"

"This is the place where they are held," came the answer. "They are all around us. Can you not sense their presence? Miriam said that she could smell them."

Paul sniffed the air. Though not as strong as in the healing place, the aroma was unmistakable. The planet smelled like bread dough, uncooked and rising. "I can smell something," he remarked. "It smells like yeast."

"Then you, too, can sense them as does the Chosen One," answered the creature. "Come walk with us."

The Children started to walk with the comedic gait that he and Borthid had noticed on arrival at the embarkation point. Paul followed. It felt good to be in the open air.

"Is this the valley that I flew across?" asked Paul when his companion paused.

"Yes," said the creature. To Paul's surprise, the Photosynthoid dropped to its knees. It began to chant as it splayed its webbed fingers and passed his palms over the surface of the sand. Paul watched with growing curiosity as the apparent ritual gestures continued.

"What is it that you chant?" he asked.

"It is an ancient song, like the one that Miriam sang to you. I ask the Skree to receive our gift."

"Do the Skree have intelligence?" asked Paul.

"They have life. They give life. The Shadduah holds them," came an answer that sounded more like a child's riddle. "Must more be added than that to reverence them?"

Paul felt almost reprimanded, if the Children were capable of such behavior. His answer verged on being defensive. "I only meant to understand the Skree. There are many answers that I want to know, but I do not yet understand how to ask the questions."

"That gives us hope, Child," said the Children. "To us, you were so different than the Chosen One, and so like the others."

"The others?" asked Paul. "You mean, Vienna and Costance?"

"Yes them, and also the others who came in darkness." The Children seemed to focus its hands over a chosen spot, and stood. Paul instinctively rose with it wondering what was to happen next. Suddenly a stream of liquid flowed from the Children's loin area. They was urinating. Paul quickly turned away.

"Why do you turn away?" asked the Children, sensing Paul's disgust.

"It is our way to hide our immodesty," answered Paul.

"You have many customs that seem unnatural to us," came the reply. "The Skree must have *longstol* to give us our breath. It is our gift to them. They are the sharers."

Paul was feeling sick. "That's what *longstol* is?" he said.

"Yes," said the Photosynthoid. "It nourishes the Skree, and the Skree give us the gift of their breath. *Longstol* is our only gift.

It is the way in which we give life to the Skree, and the Skree give us life in return."

"Of course!" thought Paul. "It is a very simple oxygen cycle." He struggled to remember the science classes he had nearly slept through. Everything seemed backward here. The animals were the source of the oxygen, sugar, and protein. The Skree, which must be some sort of yeast or bacteria, was the source of the carbon dioxide.

"Why do you only value lives that are like your own?" came an unexpected question.

"What do you mean?" asked Paul somewhat perturbed that his thoughts had been invaded again.

"You would value the Skree if they had intelligence. When you think of us, you sometimes regard me as an *'it'*. We have heard that in your thoughts. Yet, We have intelligence. The Skree have life and they give life to us. We have life and we give life to the Skree; we have given life to you. You have shared *longstol* with the Skree. You have become a sharer of life. But you do not think that you have become connected. Why do you only value lives that are like your own?"

Paul had no answer. He remembered his earlier conversation with Costance. The Ambassador had said of the Children, "they could replace us with rabbits, in the same way we could replace them with vegetables."

"I don't know; why we are like this?" said Paul haltingly. "I suppose we want to believe that we control the connections and not that the connections feed us and keep us strong. Maybe we never learned that the Skree are also sharers and that the Shadduah hold the Skree."

"Well spoken, friend of the Chosen One," answered the Children. "The Shadduah holds all things that have life and give life, the Skree and the sparrow."

Paul stopped mid-thought. "How do you know of sparrows?" he asked.

"Do you not yet understand, Paul? You are connected, you are a sharer. We have shared with you our one gift, and you give us your breath. You have life, and you give life. You are connected."

From somewhere a flood of images poured into Paul's mind. He saw the jagged ice peaks of Cormazon, and thousands of green-winged Children soaring over the plains of Anuhar. He saw expressions of tenderness in the red eye spots of alien faces, and he saw Miriam running free waving her arms for joy and splashing through bubbling pools of warm water. He heard singing, melodious and strong like all the music he had ever heard, and yet so simple that not a word was lost. "The sun shall rise with healing in his wings."

Paul began to sing.

20

Buford felt hopeless as he sat in front of his com station. He had to find a way to get in touch with Jennifer Bertram, but it seemed a losing battle. There was no answer at her apartment, even though he let the phone ring off the hook, and redialed every ten minutes for an hour and a half. It would be like her to be at work, even in the middle of the night, but why had his message to her been returned?

In an act of final desperation, he logged into the planetary database. He executed a name search for "Jennifer Bertram". He found her *curriculum vitae* including her most recent promotion, and an unscheduled pay raise that Costance had negotiated as thanks for her work on the level 15 security codes. At the end of the entry was a note: "File update in progress. CDC852-3287"

Buford's heart started to pound. The "CDC" prefix on the reference code meant "Council for Disease Control". He exited the database and entered through the protocol maze that he and Jennifer had devised for those with access above level 15. Most codes were alphanumeric, but Jennifer had suggested that time be added as a third dimension. Every number and letter in the sequence could be correct, and the user would not be able to gain entry unless the timing of the keystrokes was also correct.

At last, Buford logged on. The proof was a blank screen with no menu or prompts. He entered in the command: *"CDC VIRUS LIST UPDATE - SEARCH CURRENT/LOCAL 'BERT'".* The CRT scrolled blank with a pulsing cursor to indicate that the files were being sorted. At last the screen filled with script. Costance held his breath:

Bert, Joshua Michael	7725-981-6452
Bert, Heather Lynn	6342-097-9429
Bertecothe, Salvador O.	8935-284-7632
Bertolotti, Andrew	7394-658-7206
Bertram, Jennifer Kathryn	0429-472-8346
Bertrum, Goeffrey Kyle	8657-927-9578
Bertsrazzi, Angela Romaine	7935-746-5340

---7 matches found---

Costance could not believe his eyes. He entered another command: *"DELETE 0429-472-8346".* The prompt flashed at him, *"Processing information. Please wait."*

"Damn it! I don't want to wait," he said shouting into the screen.

At last, the machine swapped messages. *"Unable to complete deletion, current Discontinueds have been notified of treatment options."*

Costance brought his fist down on the keyboard creating a stream of gibberish on the monitor followed by the words "*Command Unknown*". He regained his composure. "My access at this level will be monitored," he reminded himself. "I need to log off and think this through." He followed the correct procedure to exit the protocol maze, and powered down the station.

He took a deep breath and began to lay out his thoughts. Jennifer had been notified of her infection by the *x-virus*. She may have gone to a treatment center, but equally possible was the fact that she may have gone home with a friend or to visit family. Buford realized how little he knew about this woman that he was about to invite to share a new home on a new planet. He didn't really know if she had a family. He searched his memory of every conversation. She had said something once about a brother, but Costance couldn't remember if he lived in the city or not.

The urgency of the present collapsed his memory. "Okay," he thought. "It's still early. She may be somewhere scared to death, but the virus is nonsense. There's no danger there. Tomorrow I'll go to her work; someone there will know how to get in touch with her."

He was not sure if he would tell her the truth about the virus. That knowledge would be deadly in and of itself. Costance finally decided that he would explain that he would use his connections to get her on the ground floor of the most promising drug for remission. At worst, he would have to supply her with placebos for the rest of her life. At best, he might get the CDC to have her retested for the virus and grant her a clean bill of health. His mind stopped racing. He went to the sideboard in his dining room and poured himself a drink of single malt scotch from a crystal decanter. He raised his glass in a toast. "To you, Jennifer Bertram; and to our getting out of here. You are the one thing worth saving." He downed the whole glass.

21

Buford did not sleep at all during the night, but it was not dread that robbed him of rest. Instead, he was overwhelmed by a burst of energy. His mind was alive and working on many levels. A door had opened to him, and his resolve to walk through that door would not falter.

Quan and Wallerton had thought that David Jahren was the major threat to their control of the planet. On this night Buford

Costance had given a new name to the threat, and it was his own. Years of loyalty had prepared him well for the rebellion, and his own meticulous scrutiny of demographics told him who his potential allies were.

While he mourned the loss of Jahren, he also knew that there were contacts to an underground on the research team that shared the discovery of the planet Galcon. It would not take much to bring these intellectuals into the fold. Buford could imagine their outrage at learning the simple truth that the *x-virus* was a non-existent enemy.

Costance knew enough about history to know that this revolution would require different armaments than those of a violent junta, but the result would be equally violent. Armed squads taking over broadcast studios would be replaced by simple electronic jamming devices to block the initiating signals for the phasings of the Ceretraks.

Those addicted to the Quan/Wallerton Group would go to the streets. The Jahrens and Bertrams of the planet, the unaddicted 8%, would have to brace for the eruption of unequalled chaos.

"In the moment of chaos, the planet will be reborn," said Costance to himself. When he realized that he had spoken the words aloud, a spasm gripped his whole body. He had no way of knowing that his apartment was not as open to the surveillance of the Council as was the holding area where Jahren had unknowingly misspoken and sealed his own doom. After a moment, peace washed over him. His resolve was greater than his fear.

The beautiful thing was that Quan and Wallerton had given him the weapon that he needed to disrupt the operation of the Ceretraks. He was assigned to surreptitiously install an identification beacon on every craft capable of even low level orbit. Such a device could easily contain a chip that would provide jamming capabilities for the Ceretrak millifrequencies. Quan and Wallerton could activate any of the units to identify a particular type of craft and its location, but Costance would be able to throw the switch on a network of jamming stations and cover most of the surface of the planet.

At first, the prospect of slipping thousands of devices on board ships without the consent or knowledge of the crew seemed daunting, but the solution was quite simple. With all the variety of ships and propulsion systems, a common feature was that all of them used fissionable resin-impregnated batteries to supply back-up power to on-board systems. Even with that, the size, shape, and ampere ratings of the power packs varied from craft to craft and manufacturer to manufacturer. There was, however, only one approved supplier of casings for the radioactive resins. That was the key to Costance's plan. New casings would be manufactured with small transmitters embedded in the shielding material. They would function like Emergency Position Indicating Radio Beacons (EPIRBs) which were used in the twenty-first century to locate ships at sea. Like the EPIRBs, their signals would automatically be relayed by the orbiting weather satellites. Once activated, the planet would be bombarded with signals to disrupt every phasing and deny the Ceretrak to the millions of addicts that relied on it. Powering the jamming devices would not be a problem. They would lie dormant within the cell casings until remotely activated. When triggered, they would draw power for transmissions from the fissionable resins in the battery like a parasite drawing strength from an unwitting host.

Costance was feeling confident in his plan, and felt a rush of energy that surpassed the loss of a night's sleep. He brewed a pot of coffee, and poured himself a cup. Pulling an afghan off his settee, he wrapped it over his shoulders and went out on his balcony. The sun was just lifting itself above the eastern edge of the city. A vaporous moon was being forced to surrender its borrowed light to the dawn. In that moment, he felt himself a child of the universe. He sipped the steaming coffee. He knew that it was his life that was dawning. Today he would trade duty for self-determination. He would find a sanctuary against the coming chaos in the heavens with Jennifer Bertram safe at his side. They would travel the skies together, and return to bring reason to a grateful people.

22

"What happened to me?" asked Paul.

"You have seen the world through eyes that are not your own," said the Children. "Did it frighten you?"

"No," answered Paul. "I did see places, and I saw Miriam. But that couldn't be. She is in the place of healing. Or did she awaken? Did I see a vision or something that is happening now?"

"It is too much for you to understand at one time, Child," came a calm response. "Let us help you to see. Do you remember the healing place?"

"Yes," said Paul. "I remember seeing Borthid. I remember the smell. The Skree were there!"

"Yes, they were in the sands. They are very strong in the place of healing. But now, we want you to go to the place of healing. Do not try to remember the place as something in the past, but try to see it now."

Paul closed his eyes. He tried to force the memory of the place into his mind, but his memory held gaps.

"Call to the Children," said his companion.

Paul did not understand the request, but in his mind he turned as if to one standing next to him. Suddenly he was not standing on the sands of the valley floor. He was standing under the crystal dome of the healing place. The strong smell of the Skree returned to his nostrils. He glanced quickly side to side to get his bearing. He spotted the distant form of Borthid lying still on the divan. Next to her was another form, a man who appeared to be asleep.

"Who is that?" asked Paul.

"Do you not recognize yourself?" echoed a chorus of voices.

"But that's not possible," said Paul, stepping closer. "How can I be here and there at the same moment?" He looked at the sleeping man, the man with his features. He had never seen anything but a two-dimensional image of himself, and he could not make this form look like his familiar reflection.

"That is the body of Paul, the friend of the Chosen One," came an unequivocal answer. "If it does not seem possible that it is you, perhaps it is not you."

"Not me?" asked Paul to himself. He opened his eyes and

was in the daylight of the valley floor. The Children was still standing next to him. "If it was me, could it be that I was seeing an image of the past, when I was still there, asleep?"

The Children smiled. Paul had never noticed facial expressions on the Children before. "No, Paul," the Children answered. "What you see is the now. The part of you that needs rest is sleeping, but you are here."

"Does that mean that when I saw Borthid running, that was also the now, and the reason I couldn't awaken her was that she was not really there?" asked Paul.

"You begin to understand," came the reply. "Walk with us." The creature began to lumber down the face of the dune. Paul followed.

The two crossed into the trough between the dunes. The newly-awakened consciousness within him made the alien landscape seem familiar. Paul was not surprised when his feet began to slosh through tepid water at the lowest point in the ravine. He looked down at the bubbly froth, and the smell of the Skree stirred all around him. They started to climb the opposite dune. The wet sands were firm under his step. Each step higher was a step to drier levels of grittiness. Paul felt his feet slipping away beneath the sliding silicon. At one point his footing failed altogether, and he found himself kneeling knee-deep in warm sand. With a simple turn, he pivoted to sit on the dune.

"I'll trade you for your feet," said Paul without thinking as the Children easily scaled the shifting earth with their broad webbed-feet. To Paul's surprise and his own embarrassment, the Children laughed with a thousand voices.

"You honor us with your humor," said the Children.

"I didn't mean to make fun of you," recovered Paul. "It's just that walking in this place is difficult for me. I guess I spoke without thinking."

"It is with friends that one can speak without thinking, and still be safe," said the creature. The Photosynthoid sat down on the ridge next to him. The Children unfolded its wings and stretched them wide, forming a great covering canopy. Paul was amazed at the massive wingspan. The sudden shade felt good, and he realized that he was drained by the heat.

"When we came here," began Paul, "we were afraid to speak to you. We were told that we couldn't make the sound of the letter 'R' when we spoke. I was afraid when Borthid spoke to you, and you took her away."

"Yes," said the Children. "We knew your fear, but the Chosen One was not afraid to speak, for she knew us as we are. You carried a fear that was given to you by others. We, too, were told to avoid the sound of the consonant so as not to offend you humans."

"That's not true," protested Paul.

"We knew that," continued the Children. "It was a rule imposed to let you live with the uncertainty of fear."

"Who did that?" asked Paul. "It's so stupid. We spent hours trying to change our speech out of fear of you."

"Do you think that we are so harmless that we should not be feared?"

Paul was perplexed. "I guess I just feel safe, maybe for the first time in my life. I do not fear that you would hurt me."

"That is because you have passed through the darkness. Otherwise, you would fear us. Your ambassador senses many things, and is wise to fear us."

"Was it he who made up that rule?" asked Paul.

"Yes," said the Children.

"I do not like him or trust him," confided Paul.

"He is himself," came the answer. "Remember that you asked us once if we *liked* you? What was our answer?"

"You said that I am Paul and I have life and I give life," answered Paul. "It sounded very odd to me."

"As did your question to us," said the creature. "Just now you said that you did not like the one called Buford Costance.

He is, however, just himself. He gives life and he has life. He is much like you."

"No!" protested Paul. "He is not at all like me. He deals in fear, and seeks only power for himself."

"But you and he are connected. Even now, you have the power to know his mind. He is afraid of the wrong things, but it is pain that makes him blind. He should be afraid of the Children, but he fears you more. That is why he will seek to kill you."

"And you still wonder why I don't like him?" said Paul with growing incredulity in his voice. He turned to face the Photosynthoid, but he was no longer on the dunes beneath the towers of the place of healing. He was in an office, looking into a cubicle, a work space. A man was seated in a swivel desk chair. The man turned his round face toward Paul. It was Buford Costance.

"What are you doing here, Orfin? I thought you were out trying to find your playmate," said Costance with a tone that defined disgust.

"Where is this place?" asked a confused Paul. Costance melted into uncontrollable sobs. The tears stopped as he redirected his pain toward hate. "You are in my damn brain, bastard!" he croaked at Paul. "You are in a memory that I hate, but will never forget. But it's my memory. Get out!"

Paul was aware that they were not alone. Standing next to him was a pleasant looking young woman. She pushed her glasses up where they had slipped down her freckled nose.

"Tell him that Jennifer is here," she said.

Paul did not pretend to understand, but he took the risk. "Jennifer is here with me," he said.

Buford sat bolt upright. "What the hell do you think you mean by coming here and saying that?" Costance rose to his feet with clenched fists.

"Ask him if the level 15 security codes still work," said Jennifer quickly.

"She asks if the level 15 security codes are still working?" said Paul. Costance froze.

"Tell him that I laughed when he drank a toast to me, and said I was the only thing on the planet worth saving," continued Jennifer. Paul relayed the message, and Costance dropped back into the chair.

"But I didn't save her," confessed Costance. "I killed her with a virus that doesn't exist."

Paul turned to face the woman next to him. "Who are you?" he asked. Before she could answer, Paul knew. She was Jennifer Bertram, and that she had died soon after being notified that she had contracted the deadly virus that had infected Borthid and himself.

"What do you mean, 'a virus that doesn't exist'?" said Paul, turning back to Costance.

"Just what I said," snapped Buford. "The damn virus, that you *Discontinueds* carry, doesn't exist."

"But people die if not treated," protested Paul.

"No, fool," said Buford. "That's what they wanted you to believe. The symptoms, the deaths, the infertility, it all came from the treatments."

"Why?" was Paul's only response.

"Simply because you didn't love the machine more than your own pathetic lives. Is Jenny really there?"

"Yes, she is," answered Paul.

"Tell her that I am so sorry," begged Costance.

"She can hear you, Buford," said Paul surprised that he called the Ambassador by his given name. Paul turned to Jennifer, but she was gone. The sun was shining over the dunes while the wind swirled the loose sand like the froth of gigantic whitecaps in turbulent seas.

"Was that real, Paul?" asked the Children.

"I think so," said Paul in a confused tone. "Did I just meet someone who is dead?"

23

Mirabella Quan was waiting impatiently in QR-4 for Blane Wallerton to make their 4 p.m. appointment. In her hand she held a ram micro disk with the latest report from Buford Costance. She resented the fact that she could not access the information without Wallerton's codes, but that was the deal the two had struck. All data was sealed electronically until both were present to read it. Quan and Wallerton had agreed that mutual distrust was the basis of their successful relationship.

There was a sudden change of pressure as the seal on the door opened. Wallerton entered.

"I'm sorry, Quan," he began. "The com stations were all activated with a national warning bulletin, and I wanted to see how it was carried."

"Was it Costance's bombshell," said Mirabella, "the news of the battery recall?"

"Yes, and I expected all hell to break loose when the news hit, but Buford thinks that there will be no more than a day's loss of any ship in the fleet," said Blane.

"What were the specifics?" urged Quan.

"Well, it didn't say that there has been any widespread contamination. Instead, it stressed that manufacturing defects in the resin-fusion units issued in the last two years posed an immediate threat. The defects were supposedly caught in the government's efficient testing program, and no incidents have been actually observed. It went on, however, to say that the breakdown would be nearly instantaneous, and an onboard incident would mean the loss of every life on the ship. The announcement was really quite alarming. It scared me, and I knew it was a crock!" Blane smiled and gave Mirabella a knowing wink.

"Did they make reference to the exchange program?" asked Quan.

"Yes, didn't you hear the planet's collective sigh of relief?" joked Blane. "The government will bear all replacement costs and adequate stocks are on hand for immediate correction of the problem. It's going to cost us a bundle."

"But the alternatives are even more frightening," added Mirabella. "I suppose we should have an investigation as to why the original casings were defective. I mean, we designed the specifications. Reports of a major flaw, imaginary or not, will reflect on us."

"Unless," pondered Blane, "unless, the defect was sabotage by some anarchist group. Then, if the beacon identification modules were uncovered, we would have a reasonable explanation as to why they had to be installed. It would be an emergency system to detect hostile craft."

Quan picked up on his train of thought. "We also might find evidence that officials in the industry were involved in the sabotage."

"Anyone particular in mind?" asked Wallerton.

"Costance gave away a whole lot of phasing privileges to quiet those who knew or could potentially figure out what had been done in the manufacturing process. Their names could match our list of terrorists. Convicting them of treason would be a death sentence. That would keep them quieter than Costance's little incentive program," observed Quan.

"Speaking of Costance, what is the word from the future ambassador to hell?" chuckled Wallerton.

"I was waiting for your codes," said Quan. "If you just let me know them, I could have a formal briefing ready for you, Representative Wallerton."

"No, thank you, Representative Quan," replied Blanc. "I don't mind reading it for myself and waiting for your oral interpretation later." The two snickered in unison.

Quan placed the micro disk in the drive of the scramble reader. She entered her codes swiftly and accurately, then stepped back to let Wallerton enter his. She turned away as if giving him privacy. Inwardly she smiled at the fact that she knew every digit that he was entering on the keyboard. One day she might have to pull his strings in a little tighter, and she had prepared a few surprises of her own. So far, however, he was still somewhat amusing.

The monitor came to life as Blane finished the code sequence. He slid two blank disks into the other drives. Once the master was accessed, copies of the reports would be sent as secure files to the other disks so that Quan and Wallerton could view them privately. Quan stepped to Wallerton's side to read the text:

TO: Representatives Quan and Wallerton
FROM: B. Costance
RE: Special assignments

I'm beginning with this one page summary, but complete supporting documents are appended for further study. Here are the main highlights:

Resin-fusion battery recall: The recall should be initiated by the time you read this report. The new casings are fitted with transmission devices. Because the batteries vary from craft to craft, I was able to modify the frequencies for each battery size and capacity. In short, when activated, the signals will provide a configuration to tell us the exact type of vessel. I have also been assured that both satellite and earth stationed missiles could lock on to such signals and destroy the target.

Pod production: The first prototype has lived up to every expectation. It is, in fact, fully operational and virtually indestructible. The gas jets are very efficient, and will not only provide steering for the main trek, but docking capabilities on the planet itself. The genetically engineered hydrogen/oxygen harvesters have proven very efficient. The pods can be produced at the rate of two a month, once approval is given.

Crew readiness: The crew is ready! I've never seen people so excited. They are all volunteers. The actual training has been simple. The navigating is done by the on-board computers, and the crew is along for the ride. The course that has been plotted seems so foolproof, that they say anyone could make the journey, if they can endure the cramped quarters. (The Ceretraks should handle that detail.)

The subway: The return trip seems to be of some concern. Obviously Jahren thought it possible, for there is nothing about it in his documentation. Some think that the heat buildup will be too great inside the pod. The speed projections are phenomenal. It'll take nine months to get there, but less than three to return. Some theorists are predicting a time warp at that speed so that if the crew were to go to Galcon, harvest the gases, and immediately launch for the return, they could actually arrive back here at about the time that they left.

Other matters: Might I suggest another strategy? If the retrieval of returning pods is a concern, why not hedge your bets by having shuttles available to the returning crews? For instance, suppose we position a shuttle in orbit, give it the electronic signature of an inactive satellite, and power its on-board systems with some of the old battery packs? It will not be detectable. In a worst case scenario, the pods could dock with it, and the crew could be self-rescuing. It could foil any pirates. It is just a suggestion.

The two looked up from the document, and burst out laughing.

"Do you think that Ambassador Costance is getting worried about the return trip?" asked Wallerton in a mocking tone. "I say that we offer him peace of mind, and approve his ideas with commendation."

"There's no telling who might need a shuttle, and it may just fit our need better than our original plan," said Quan.

"Then we are in agreement," concluded Wallerton.

24

Paul sat in silence beneath the wings of the Children. The winds began to roar outside the covering protection of the Photosynthoid.

"It is the time of no shadows," whispered the creature. Paul remembered the phenomenon when he flew over the valley. The suns were at their greatest strength, each erasing the shadows of the other. "You must sleep now," advised the Children. Paul needed no coaxing. His head was still swimming from the encounter with Costance and the appearance of Jennifer Bertram.

He stretched out on the warm sand which gave way to the shape of his body. He propped his head on his outstretched arm, and was asleep before the Children began to sing of the gifts of wind and suns, and the Shadduah who holds the Skree.

Paul had not dreamed since he was a boy, at least not with any remembrance that he could carry into the daylight. Suddenly, however, the skies over Galcon were full of stars.

"I had forgotten the stars," he said aloud.

"How could you forget them?" came a familiar voice. It was Borthid. He did not know whether the planet grew suddenly smaller, or he so much larger, but now the two were on the *Renegade*.

"Where did you come from?" Paul asked. Borthid smiled with mischief in her eyes.

"What do you mean, *Where did I come from?*" she answered. "We've been in this pod for nearly nine months. Tomorrow we'll be on Galcon."

"Are you scared?" asked Paul.

"Scared?" she said, pausing. "No, Orfin, I am not scared. For the first time in my life I feel like I belong somewhere." Borthid began her exercise routine, counting leg-lifts to keep the muscles in tone.

"I'm not sure I would know what that feels like," said Paul.

"I think you are where you belong, Orfin," she consoled. "Your singing has certainly improved." He felt his face flush.

"I didn't know how to sing before," he said.

"How could you not know how to sing?" she teased. "You just have to listen, and then allow your heart to follow."

"You've got to have a heart first," said Paul. "A voice helps, too."

Borthid looked sideways at him as she switched legs for her exercise. "You have a good voice," she said. "You have a big heart, too. You just don't look at yourself that way anymore."

Paul wondered why she said '*anymore*'. Had he ever felt anything? He was afraid to think about it. His emotions seemed a collection of feelings that one was *supposed* to feel. Love the people who love you. Hate the people who hate you. When confused, hurt, or scared, lash out in anger. Those were the rules he had been taught. They worked. If they left you empty, well, who said life was to be more than that anyway?

"When did you get so cynical?" asked Borthid as though she could read his mind. Orfin didn't know whether she expected an answer or not. In any case, he had none to give her.

Paul watched her complete her exercise routine. "Orfin, can I ask a really big favor of you?"

"Sure," he said automatically.

"I don't want to use that Ceretrak on the planet. It wouldn't be right. I know how silly that sounds, but it belongs to a different place."

Paul paused to think. He could not understand the request, but he was beginning to feel something. He was beginning to feel that Borthid's insights were truer than his own. "Sure," he said, as though it were an easy thing.

Borthid smiled. "Thank you, Paul."

Had she called him Paul? Did she name him before he had spoken his own name in the darkness? Paul could not remember if he was in a dream or in reality. Borthid seemed real enough. He stared at her until she became aware of it.

"What?" she asked. Until she spoke, he was not aware that he wanted to say anything. "Were you going to say something?" she invited.

There was a stirring of the sand, and Paul began to wake up. The haziness of sleep began to erase the image of his mind. "I love you," he said with a lump in his throat. He was awake, and sitting on the ridge of a dune. The Children were winging high overhead, and a pale shadow stretched out in front of him.

25

Buford Costance was clearly shaken. He went to his private stock of scotch and poured himself a liberal dose. It had been bad enough when he had realized that the Froggies could read thoughts; they were harmless enough and disinterested in earth politics. When Orfin appeared inside his brain, he envisioned ruin to his scheme. How had the *Discontinued* mastered that skill so quickly? Of most significance, how did Orfin know the name of Jennifer Bertram?

"Timing is everything," he thought, "especially in comedy and insurrection." Orfin and Borthid had obviously been able to leave the earth's solar system before the computer-activated jamming had come on-line. He racked his brain to unscramble the chaos of comparing time sequences between Earth and Galcon. Were his calculations correct? He wished Jenny had been able to check them on her computer. He could only hope that his *alarm clock* would ring on time. The name of his wake up call was Vienna. As he was rethinking the problem, she walked through the door.

"Cosy, is it about time?"

"No, Vienna," he answered, trying not to show his disgust. "The phasing can't happen for another ten minutes."

"How about the ones you got from those sick people?" she asked.

"They are not sick, Vienna. That was just a scheme we made up about them. You used both their phasings half an hour ago. Remember, you put a wrist ring on each hand?"

"Oh, yeah, that was nice. When can I do that again?"

"That won't be possible for another five and a half hours," answered Buford doing the simple calculations. "Vienna, sit down." Vienna sat down, for all the world looking like a pouting five year old. Her eyes wandered about the room, unable to focus on the Ambassador, or on anything else.

"Vienna," began Costance. "Vienna, do you remember that pretty soon the phasings are going to stop?"

"But you could fix it, couldn't you, Cosy?" she pleaded.

"Not right away, Vienna. Remember I told you that when your wrist rings stop working, that will be the signal that the earth's system has been shut down for ten months. Then we'll get back on our ship and go back home very fast. It's hard to understand, but when we get back, no one on the earth will have had a phasing for one month."

"Won't people be upset?" asked Vienna.

"Yes, Vienna," said Constance trying to explain his plan for the hundredth time. "We know they'll be upset. After we get back, I will start the phasings again, and you and I will be heroes."

"Cosy?"

"Yes, Vienna?"

"Is it about time?" Buford looked at his watch.

"I suppose you could get ready," answered Costance.

"I don't have to, Cosy," said Vienna. "I just wear all the wrist wrings all the time. It saves me time. Isn't that good planning, Cosy?"

"Actually, the phasings won't start until the frequency pulses reach the planet," explained Costance. He looked at her blank expression. "Yes, that's good planning, Vienna." She smiled, and got up to go. Costance didn't have to ask where. She was going to the sunlit atrium where the presence of the Froggies enriched the oxygen content.

"This place is hell," thought Costance. "I've plotted every contingency for the restoration of the Earth, and I have an idiot as my only collaborator." He recalled the day he had asked Quan and Wallerton to approve Vienna as his first choice for the diplomatic team. Even then he knew that he needed her to take all the phasings required to keep him and Jenny off the list of suspicious people. The plan would have worked, had he not offered Jenny an unscheduled promotion. When the computer-generated list of non-phasers was cross-referenced with the list containing the unscheduled promotions, her name had surfaced. The combination meant ambitious and non-addictive, and placed her on the list of those prescribed for toxic treatment. Quan and Wallerton felt that having people occasionally die within days or hours of diagnosis was a graphic reminder of the power of the virus. When Costance pulled strings to get a promotion for a woman he admired, he had signed her death warrant.

"God," he said. "I'd give up everything for a ten minute conversation with Jenny." His mind went back to the moment when Orfin had invaded his thoughts. He had been thinking of the morning when he had visited Jenny's office, the morning that everyone was informed of her sudden death. While reliving the torture of that moment, Orfin had appeared mentioning her name. Something was happening, and he feared that Orfin and Borthid were spies sent by Quan and Wallerton. How else would they have known about Jenny?

If Orfin had now mastered the Photosynthoids' techniques, they could soon discover that he and Vienna were waiting to ride the *cosmic subway* back to Earth's solar system. They would use their pod to dock with one of the two unidentifiable shuttles that he had left in orbit, just as Wallerton and Quan had done when pirates went after their pod. Even if the earth-based missiles shot down every satellite and ship that was sending a jamming signal, his escape shuttles would be safe. They were retrofitted with older versions of the resin-fusion batteries. In fact, if every sensor and ship were blown out of orbit, it would be all the better. From their vantage point in space, they would be able to determine the chaos, and reestablish phasings to bring stability back to the planet.

Costance tried to drive all thoughts from his head. He did not want Orfin to appear again in order to raid his consciousness. He tried to think of Vienna, but the thought of her was too repulsive to sustain.

26

"The cost of this project may be getting out of control," said Blane.

"Why do you say that?" asked Quan.

"Did you see this list of supplies that Costance has requested?" complained Wallerton. "He wants a pulse accelerator to send signals faster than light speed. We already have committed one to the project and it's on-line."

"But he doesn't know about that one," reminded Quan. "Does he say what it is for?"

"Yes, he's very specific. He wants it for both data communication and for transmission of phasing cues."

"That makes sense," said Mirabella. "That's what we're using it for. I'm surprised that he hasn't tried to make the argument that he be permitted to generate the Ceretrak millifrequencies on Galcon. If the signals are sent from Earth, it will provide us with some cross-galactic control. He's playing right into our hands. Why don't we just offer him the one that's already on-line? In a few days it'll be public knowledge anyhow."

"You mean when the triumphant explorers return from Galcon?" said Blane with a wink and a smile.

"Why, Blane Wallerton, when everyone knows that we traveled across the universe together sharing our phasings, we will be the talk of the planet." Quan's voice took on an unusually playful tone.

"At least we hope so," added Blane. "Fortunately we've had enough experience in the quiet rooms that I can describe your responses if the tabloids want a real story."

"And turnabout would be fair play, remember that!" said Quan. "I could make up something about your romping with the amphibians on Galcon, you animal!" The two laughed.

"That was the biggest surprise," added Blane. "Who'd have guessed that we'd discover sentient beings, harmless ones at that! In some ways, it may make it easier to send people out there. The environment is not as hostile as might have been the case. Food supplies are not dependent on establishing agriculture. So as long as the creatures are docile and welcoming, we actually have a place to send our one-way travelers."

"It was a good idea to send out the first team of explorers without an announcement," said Quan. "If the mission had failed, well, we could try again publicly. This way we will prove to the world that the place is habitable and the return is safe. We'll be the living proof, the pioneers who inaugurated a new Age of Discovery."

"And," noted Wallerton, "if anyone has been monitoring signals from deep space, they can confirm that coded messages have been coming from Galcon to the Planetary Council. Wait until they find out who steps out of the returning pod."

"I plan to be there to see that!" said Quan.

"I'll be right behind you, partner," said Wallerton.

"In the meantime, do I tell Costance that he'll get his accelerator?"

"Why not?" said Blane. "Just make sure that you route our response through Galcon. He's crafty enough to figure out our plan. If our communications with him don't match the deep-space signals, it'll be a dead giveaway. I'll sure feel better when we can say that we have an Ambassador on Galcon."

"Especially if that Ambassador is Buford Costance," remarked Quan.

As the two were talking, an urgent message came over the jury- rigged com station in the corner of the small hotel room. Wallerton went to the console and activated the chat mode.

"It's from the Captain of the *Mongoose*. They've been monitoring the satellite observation data, and there's been a disturbance in the sector where we expect the pod to emerge."

"It's at least a day and a half earlier than predicted," said Quan. "Is he sure?"

"Of course he's not sure, it has no metallic content, and a positive identification from conventional tracking mechanisms is highly unlikely. But there has been some unexpected space distortion, and the pod is the most likely explanation. I think we'd better get ourselves to the shuttle."

"I can't say that I'm sorry to leave the squalor of this fleabag place," stated Quan. "It's been a long two weeks, and I'm sure we've kept everyone guessing as to our whereabouts. In a few hours, the world will have an answer. Of course, the answer will be wrong. When they hear we've been on Galcon, nobody will suspect that we've been holed up in a third rate motel."

It was raining when the two left the motel and made their way along the perimeter of the county shuttle port. By ducking through a jagged opening in the chain-link fence, they cut some distance off their journey. They passed four dilapidated craft along the edge of the concrete pad. The rain was pelting them as they saw the *Mongoose* sitting in the launch position where it had been for a week.

"Remember our deal, Wallerton," said Quan. "No names are to be mentioned. This is a no-questions-asked cash deal."

As they approached the sleek craft, they could hear the jet engines whirring. The *Mongoose* was an early hybrid class jet/shuttle, an atmospheric shuttle capable of short excursions into near space. As they crossed in front of the ship, they caught a glimpse of a red glow in the mid-section of the starboard side.

The hatch was open. The inside of the craft was dimly lit with a red light to prevent night blindness. A figure was crouching just inside. Quan and Wallerton approached the short boarding ladder. Blane gave a wave of recognition and started up into the companionway. Mirabella followed.

No words were spoken until the hatch was sealed by the guard who had been watching their approach.

"Do you have the coordinates?" said the sentry. Quan handed him a laser cassette.

"As instructed," she said.

Everyone on the four-person crew seemed curious. The two felt under intense scrutiny. Quan wondered whether they had been recognized until Wallerton leaned over to whisper to her. "It's our coveralls," he said.

Mirabella realized that he was right. Not many clandestine passengers ever appear in the baggy, reflective togs of the Center for Interplanetary Exploration. They strapped themselves in the two unoccupied g-seats. Both Quan and Wallerton were trained in shuttle navigation and piloting, and had no trouble fastening themselves in the inflatable seats that would protect them from the thrust pressures they would encounter while escaping the earth's gravity.

A woman's voice came from the cockpit. It was the Captain.

"This storm hit just in time," she said. "This is good pirate weather; we can skip the aircraft avoidance routine."

A mumbled acknowledgement was heard from somewhere. A moment later the ship began to shake until Wallerton feared that it would shatter. It didn't. The proof was that they felt the g-seats inflate around them, and the mounting pressure squeezing the blood through their screaming arteries.

When they had recovered from blacking out, Quan and Wallerton realized that the crew was busy preparing the docking mechanism. They moved skillfully in the weightless environment. "I believe we've sighted the pod you've asked us to recover," said the Captain. "It's just off the port beam."

Blane looked through the Tuyere sight, and then beckoned to Quan, who also looked. The image was alarming. The charred pod was still glowing white-hot in places. The amazing thing, however, was that its hull integrity seemed to be intact. Obviously Jahren had been correct about the survivability of the design, but the contents had to have been incinerated.

"We'll have to let that cool before it can be brought into the hold," said the Captain. "Now we'll have to find that shuttle that you claim is there. We'll capture that pod later."

"Good," answered Quan. She was surprised how different her voice sounded in the cabin's atmospheric mixture.

The shuttle quietly heeled and switched to a new vector. "The only signal that I can read in this sector is a disabled COSPAS/SARSAT satellite," said the Captain.

"That's it," advised Wallerton, "head for that collision beacon."

"Well, I'll be damned!" said a technician, drawing glances from the others of the crew for breaking his silence. Quan looked through the sight glass. It was there. Instead of the expected solar array of a communications satellite, it was an unmarked shuttle, one of the constellation class.

The pilot brought the *Mongoose* along side the sleeping ship. Slowly she maneuvered the craft until the docking hatches were in alignment. "On my mark," called the pilot. "Set!" A metallic clank and a shudder indicated that the link had been made. The hissing of escaping gases equalized the pressure between the ships, and the seal was broken.

"This is where we get off," said Wallerton. It had been some time since he had experienced weightlessness, but managed to slide through the connecting hatchway just behind Quan.

Once inside the dormant shuttle, Quan headed for the auxiliary power switch while Wallerton attended the resealing of the hatch. The resin-fusion batteries came on-line, and the control panels and illumination came to full strength.

Wallerton wrapped on the hatch cover to indicate to the crew of the *Mongoose* that they had powered-up and were ready to separate. They could hear the scrabble of the crew working overhead, and then nothing. If they had looked out of the sight glass, they would have seen the silent hulk of the *Mongoose* slipping by.

"They've scanned us," announced Quan.

"We knew they would," exclaimed Wallerton. "These types don't survive without being suspicious. But we're clean. There are no armaments on this ship."

"But there are on the *Mongoose*," warned Quan. "Suppose they want to double-cross us?"

"I don't think they will, not until they have some idea of what that pod may be worth," said Wallerton. "We've offered them enough to make their grandchildren rich, but payment won't be made until the pod is captured and returned to us."

"Which makes us a secure investment, doesn't it?" teased Mirabella. She slid a preconfigured communications disk into the ship's com station. "Here is your wake-up call, Ambassador Costance," she said.

"Don't send it yet," warned Blane. "Let them reach the pod."

*   *   *

Back on earth's surface, Buford Costance was startled by an emergency distress code blaring at his personal com station. More surprising was the fact that the message originated in space and was sent over his personal frequency.

> Buford.... no time for questions. I've just returned from Galcon. I've made it to the shuttle, but the pod is being hijacked. Initiate emergency sequence. Verify single jet/shuttle. Sector G, coordinates 27-65-0078. Urgent! They will soon find my location. Wallerton

The message was confirmed as Wallerton's by the code access filter which verified its origin. Costance was stunned. Wallerton had not been seen for a couple of weeks, but his being on Galcon was unbelievable.

The call was for the initiation of the emergency sequence. Costance immediately visualized the drill. First, a call had to be made to the Planetary Defense Council headquarters. Next, he would enter the authorization codes which would then be confirmed. Finally, he would enter the codes to activate the beacons in Sector G. Any vehicle in that sector would start emitting signals from the transmitters housed in their resin-fusion batteries. After that, the military would verify any battery configuration matching a jet/shuttle. Constance would be asked to enter the launch sequence authorization codes, and missiles would destroy the shuttle. Wallerton would be safe.

Constance stopped short. Did he want to do it? All his planning had been for revenge on the system imposed by Quan and Wallerton. Was he being given a free gift? A simple delay in time might suffice to fulfill his plan. Then another thought occurred to him. Quan's name was not on the note. Unless they both were removed in one operation, the survivor would be merciless. "Better to play out the whole hand," thought Costance. He logged on to the Defense Council hotline.

*   *   *

The brightness of the flash from the missile strike on the *Mongoose* surprised Quan and Wallerton. As they expected, the blast also destroyed the scorched pod and with it all the forensic evidence that would dispute the survivability of the *cosmic subway*. Landing the shuttle proved the easiest part of the journey, and a grateful planet turned out to cheer the heroes of the Galcon Expedition.

27

When Paul awoke, the Children swooped down from the sky and stood in front of him. "We must leave you for now," said the Children.

"Here?" asked Paul.

"Do not be afraid." came the reply. "Your pilgrimage requires that you walk alone for a time. We, too, must travel. But ours are the paths of the air to meet our cousins. This is a time of changes, and the Children sing together."

Paul did not pretend to understand the exact meaning of the words, but he felt urgency in the otherwise restrained speech. "Before we go," said the Children. "You must take sustenance." The Photosynthoid's webbed hands made an efficient cup. He collected *longstol* from his loin area and invited Paul to drink the life-giving fluid. It was rich and sweet. Receiving it seemed a great gift to Paul.

"Thank you," said Paul.

"You are a Sharer," responded the Creature. With that, huge wings opened and Paul felt the push of air against his cheek as the Children took to flight. Their scent brought back memories of spring days washed clean by warm rains. He stood alone.

The Orfin who arrived on the planet would have panicked on being stranded on the empty plain with no map or chart. For that part, even a good set of directions would have mattered little in the featureless land. His mind went back to his journey through the blackness, and the voice which had told him that his darkness was *a place in time and not in space.* Could not this light be a place in time? He started to walk.

At first Paul was disappointed by the terrain that was so devoid of color. It had not occurred to him that the Photosynthoids were the only variation on a planet of beige sands and translucent rock. The Children were remarkably colorful. It was their differences that provided the first shock. Their lizard-like appearance hid a great beauty. Fortunately he had learned to see deeper. The hues of their photosynthetic pigments made their appearance change like the sparkles of sunlight through the leaves of a tree. Or were they more like the spectral shapes that danced around him when his darkness was lifted?

Images were alive in Paul's mind. He walked over the crest of a dune. Below him, in the trough of the indistinguishable sandscape, a man was seated facing across the pool of the Skree.

"I've been waiting for you," said the man, turning to Paul. He seemed about Paul's age, early thirties.

Paul's heart leaped. "Who are you?" he asked.

The man laughed with a lightheartedness that made Paul

smile. "You are alone on a strange planet. You see the first of your own kind since your dream of Miriam, and you want to begin with a formal introduction!"

"I am not alone," said Paul, surprised by his own response.

"I know," said the stranger. "You never were."

"Do you know me?" asked a confused Paul. "Are we connected?"

"Yes, we are connected, Paul."

"Then how come I can't see your thoughts; you seem to know everything, my name, even my dreams?"

"I know much more than that," the man replied. "As to why you do not yet know me, perhaps you are looking in the wrong place." Paul did not know how to respond. The stranger turned away and cast a gaze over the dunes. "You were a poet once, weren't you, Paul?" the man continued. "How would you write about this place?"

Paul was surprised by the question, but it was one he could answer:

Morning star and evening star,
shadows of light on light,
I walk a world of strangeness
and yet, I am at home.

There was a period of silence. Then the stranger spoke. "I

am glad that you are still a poet. It is a gift that I admire. I too, am a writer, but my words have only brought me pain. Yours bring me peace. Thank you, Paul."

Paul was curious. He had not meant to give a gift, but the man was obviously being transformed before his eyes. Paul wanted to know more. "What did you write?" he asked.

"It was a long time ago," the stranger began. "I was sure that people were being hurt, so I wrote of freedom. I wrote the truth."

"How did that bring you pain?" asked Paul.

"There are those who cannot hear truth," came the answer. "They directed their anger at me, and the pain that I wrote about became my pain."

"Couldn't you have fought back?" challenged Paul.

"Not without becoming like them," said the man. "So I kept writing until my words became a danger to those around me. I could endure many things, but not seeing the people I love hurt by my words."

"Did you stop writing?" asked Paul.

"That was not possible for me, any more than you can stop the poetry in your own heart." The stranger seemed to drift away from the conversation. He turned away from Paul, but Paul was sure that tears were running down the man's cheek.

"So you did not stop writing. What did you do?"

"I left the people that I loved the most, and chose to live with the pain. It was the only way I could keep them safe."

"I can understand that," consoled Paul.

"I am glad that you understand," said the man. Then in a lower tone he added: "I'm glad that your mother gave you my name, and that you chose it back."

Suddenly Paul could see. He saw his mother as a young woman. Her kind smile burst into laughter, and he could hear her again. "It is now you who bring me the gift," he said. His father was gone.

28

The impact of the stranger's revelation left Paul deep in thought by the shallow wadi. He had not noticed the growing line of clouds rising up into the sky. When the first drops of rain hit his skin, his mind returned to the reality of his situation. He did not know what the rain might do in this place, so he moved to the high side of the dune. The storm struck violently, but was short-lived. As he stood in the pelting shower, Paul could see the dark cloud bank passing swiftly overhead.

Far out at the perimeter of the storm, he saw the Children

winging free in open skies. The rain ceased, and the voices of the Children came to him on the wind:

> Morning star and evening star,
> shadows of light on light,
> I walk a world of strangeness
> and yet, I am at home.

They were singing his song. Among the voices, he heard Miriam's clearly.

"Miriam," he called.

"I'm here," came her reply.

Paul turned toward the direction of her voice. She was standing just behind him. He ran to her, and threw his arms around her. "Are you alright?" he asked.

"Yes," she said. "This is a wonderful place, but I've missed your company."

"For the longest time, I was afraid that you were in danger," exclaimed Paul. "But now I think that there is no danger in this place."

"Except for the danger that we bring with us," said Miriam. The two walked together along the dune. Their hands reached for each other. "The Children say that changes and dangers are coming soon, and we must be prepared," she added.

"They told me that Costance will try to kill me," offered Paul.

"There is a lot of anger in him. I think we should go to see him, but I doubt if anything will come of it." As they walked, the waters in the trough began to rise. Miriam and Paul found themselves stranded on an island amid the flood. They sat down opposite each other, facing one another in silence.

"When you dreamed about the two of us in the *Renegade* you said that you loved me. Was that something you really meant?" asked Miriam. "You don't have to answer that," she added.

"I was surprised when I heard myself saying that," said Paul. "I have thought a lot about it since. Yes, it's true, I do love you. I didn't say it that time on the *Renegade*, because I didn't really understand what the word meant."

"There are a lot of things that seem clearer on this planet." answered Miriam.

"I feel that, too," answered Paul. "But I think that you knew that before we got here. It was in your singing on the ship. The further we got from earth, the more at peace you seemed to be. I can't understand that."

"I'm beginning to understand," said Miriam. "But you were changing, too. You began to sing with me, remember? Now your words are being sung by the Children."

"Why is that? I can't figure that out."

"Oh, Paul, can't you see who they are? They rejoice at

beauty, and your words have touched them. They have touched me. When I shared your dream, I felt your love, and I knew the rest of the truth."

"The rest of the truth?" asked Paul.

"That I love you, too," she said looking into his eyes. She placed her smooth hand against his cheek, and a single tear welled up out of his bleary eyes. She collected the droplet on her fingertips and transferred it to her own cheek. "We have shared a tear," she said. "Now I know that we are one."

"We have shared our thoughts," added Paul. "You have seen me, and yet you love me."

"It is *because* I have seen you, that I love you," said Miriam. "And I will not hide from you."

"I know," said Paul. The two embraced in tears and in laughter. They kissed deeply, and the flowing streams churned in harmony with the song of the Children.

> Morning star and evening star,
> shadows of light on light,
> I walk a world of strangeness
> and yet, I am at home.

29

It was morning, but in that land of light the passage of time is punctuated by patterns of sleeping and waking, rather than by light and dark. Paul felt Miriam stir next to him, and opened his eyes to see the light of the morning star. It would be hours before they came to the time of no shadows when the evening star appeared.

While they slept, the waters had receded, and as they stood together, the wilderness of the plain seemed more like a lush garden. The island of sand that had been so isolated by the rains, now extended as a great way across the face of the planet, or at least as far as the horizon.

"The Children once told me that I would have to cross that valley," said Paul. "I don't see how it is possible, but then they see many things that I cannot understand."

"They do see many things," agreed Miriam. "There are also many ways to cross a valley." she added, taking his hand. Paul turned to look at her as a bright flash seemed to happen all around them. Before he could question anything, Paul realized he was standing in a sunlit atrium. On his right was a corridor that he recognized. If he followed it, it would lead him to the *Renegade* or to the Ambassador's quarters and the place where he had encountered his own darkness.

Something, however, was missing. "Where are the Children?" he asked.

"Call to them, and you will see," answered Miriam. Paul realized that he was forgetting his connectedness, and that was something Miriam did not do.

He opened his mind, and silently spoke to the Children. He saw them in the dune-troughs of the great rift. They were drinking from the ponds, like a flock of birds feeding before a storm. "What are they doing?" he asked.

"They are gathering the Skree for the journey," answered Miriam, who seemed more in tune with the ways of the Children.

"Journey?" inflected Paul.

"It is the change that they have spoken of," she answered. "This place in time is soon to end, and they are preparing to leave."

"Where will they go? How will they travel?" questioned a troubled Paul.

"The Shadduah knows," Miriam answered. Paul thought she was beginning to sound like the Children. "They are now the gatherers," she continued. "They wish to bring the Sharers, and they want us to gather those of our kind."

"Costance and Vienna?" remarked Paul.

"Yes," she said.

"But he may try to kill me," Paul reminded her.

"Why does that frighten you?" The question stopped him cold, but he could not think of a single good reason why it should. The two clasped hands and walked toward the Ambassador's quarters. The portal opened to them and they entered. A surprised Costance looked up from his alcoholic stupor.

"Don't tell me you want to book passage with me for the return to earth?" he sneered. Paul wondered if he had heard the warning from the Children.

"You have no way of returning to the earth," remarked Miriam. "We have come to invite you to join us."

Costance laughed. "Don't tell me that you've both *gone native*, and, with the Froggies, no less?"

"They are not as you see them!" exclaimed Paul.

"And you aren't either," barked Costance. "You learn a native trick for some kind of telepathy; then you try to read my mind. I know who you are, though. It's too late to tell anything to your masters now." A harried Vienna entered the room. Her straggly appearance shocked Paul and Miriam.

"They still aren't working, Cosy! You said you could fix them."

"When we get back to earth!" the Ambassador snapped at her. "There's the proof," he said pointing to Vienna and turning

171

back to Paul. "The phasing cues are sent from earth by a pulse accelerator. They have stopped. I am now in my window of opportunity. The earth is in chaos, and your bosses are going to be lynched if they can't get the frequencies back on-line."

"I have no idea what you are talking about," said a confused Paul.

"Maybe I've put the wrist rings on wrong; would you check them?" Vienna whined.

"They won't work, damn it!" barked Costance. "Get out of here!"

"Maybe the Froggies can make them better; they're always nice to me," said a tearful Vienna. She ran from the room.

"Once you told me that you and Vienna were to have a child together, and you asked me to be the childer," said Miriam.

"Things change, Borthid," answered the Ambassador. "Why don't you return to earth with me? This spy can't promise you anything now."

"Paul and I have no power to make promises; we only invite you to join us. The time is changing, and our hope is with the Children."

"Then you have the hope of a fool," said Costance to Miriam. "I know more of what is happening than you do. But I can't let you waste your future with one of Quan and Wallerton's minions." He lifted the lid of a small box on the crystal table. He reached in and withdrew an old-fashioned assassin's magnum automatic. "It's an antique, made of plastic to get through airport screening" he muttered, "but it will make the point." He directed the gun at Paul and squeezed the trigger. There was a flash of light, the pungent smoke of an explosion, and a projectile passed through Paul's chest. It pierced the wall behind him with an ear-splitting crack, and left a spider's web around a hole in the crystalline partition.

When the smoke cleared, the look of surprise on Paul's face was matched only by the look on the Ambassador's. At such short range, the impact of the shot should have thrown Paul against the wall, but it did not. The bullet passed through him without harm, and apparently through the wall behind him.

"Have it your way then," he shouted as he threw the gun down. "Die in this hell hole!" Costance ran out the door, and turned toward the embarkation point where the *Renegade* was docked. They heard some commotion as he apparently slipped making the turn. "Oh, shit!" they heard him yell. Then they heard only the sound of heavy feet running away down the corridor.

"What happened?" asked Paul.

"We are here," answered Miriam. "But our bodies are still in the place of healing. He had nothing to kill."

Miriam was wrong. As they left the room, they discovered the dead form of Vienna. She was lying in the corridor where she had been struck by the bullet that passed through the wall.

30

"Call the Children," said Miriam. Paul felt himself unconsciously turn. In his perceptions, he saw concerned expressions on the faces of the Photosynthoids. They were moving toward them.

"Do not be afraid," said the Children in a single voice.

Paul and Miriam looked down on the quiet body of Vienna lying in a pool of blood. As they stood, the Children joined them. In the background of their consciousness, they heard the engines of the *Renegade* firing.

"He is now truly alone," said Miriam, breaking the silence.

"I wonder if he will find what he is looking for when he gets back?" asked Paul

"But he won't get back," stated a man standing among the Children. Paul and Miriam looked over and saw Dr. David Jahren. "There never was a path that he could follow that would carry him to his revenge."

"What are you talking about?" asked Miriam. In a moment, Paul and Miriam saw the Doctor before the Planetary Council. In his memory and through his eyes, they could see the interest in the eyes of one particular man and woman. The saw the knowing glances that passed between Mirabella Quan and Blane Wallerton. They also saw Buford Costance extending a friendly greeting and entering the lift. They felt the air being knocked from their lungs and the falling into darkness. They knew the man who was speaking to them.

"I warned them all that the trip back to earth would be impossible," he concluded. "But I didn't know what was in their hearts."

They all stood in silence, looking at Vienna.

"Who was she?" asked Jahren.

"She was another victim," offered Paul. "We cannot know who she would have been if she had claimed her life as her own."

"She was herself," said the Children. "She had life and she gave life."

"But she really didn't have a chance," protested Miriam. "She..." She broke off her speech mid-thought. "You are right," she added. "She had life and she gave life. She was a Sharer."

Paul and Miriam could never adequately describe what

followed. As bright as the corridor had been, the space paled when compared to a new light that surrounded them. What appeared as brightness a moment before, now seemed like the mist of clouds. Through the clouds streaked salvoes of light which converged to become one. Miriam took Paul's hand. He turned to look at her, but her eyes were turned toward the newer light that reflected off her face until it looked as though she, too, was a source of illumination. Miriam began to sing. "The Sun shall rise with healing in its wings."

Paul watched in quiet wonder. Through the luminescence, he saw the movement of light within light, and the place where Vienna's body had lain became a dissolving shadow. Her form dissipated in glowing. He could never tell whether she had stood up in the midst of that shining, or whether the Children had carried her. Whichever was the case, in that moment the chorus had stopped. The body of Vienna was gone. He and Miriam were alone. She was looking into his eyes, and she could see him as he was. He saw her too, and he loved her.

After a peaceful silence and their joined hands ceased tender caressing, Paul spoke. "What just happened?"

"You saw the Children as they are," answered Miriam. "It is the way that I saw them the first day in the atrium. They need the light of the suns, but the light that they carry in themselves is far greater."

"How come I could not see them that way?" asked Paul.

"You were not ready," answered Miriam. "Come with me," she said leading him toward the sunlit atrium. They sat on a crystal divan facing each other. Paul thought Miriam was about to speak when she leaned toward him and kissed him tenuously on his lips. He found himself kissing her back. They embraced. Their bodies felt wondrously warm and familiar, and all sense of time passed to oblivion as they touched and were touched, as they made love and felt love.

When they were at peace, they wandered through each other's thoughts. Miriam spoke with Paul's mother on a sunny afternoon when a small boy fished by a lake, and with his father by a pool of Skree on Galcon. Paul held hands with Miriam's mother when the attendant took away the child she bore for an *Alpha*. He wiped a tear from the cheek of a young girl who watched her mother strap on wrist rings. That tear brought them both to the moment on the dune when Miriam had taken a tear from his cheek.

"We are walking the same path, Paul," she said. It was the truth.

"And it seems that we are going to walk it here, on Galcon," was his answer.

"No," she said. "This is a place in time. It is the time we were to meet, but it cannot be the place where we shall stay."

"But we know that we cannot get back," he argued.

"I do not understand either," answered Miriam. "This is the time we must trust the Children, for they have sung their song before the Shadduah. They know another path."

As they spoke, another sound came to them from a distance. The message was familiar in words and tone. It was the recorded voice of Buford Costance: "This is the embackation point. You will be geeted by the cuewent ambassidoe at the end of the passage. You may encountoo Photosynthoids enwoute. Please weefane fum vocal communications until following you beefing."

"What triggered that?" asked Paul.

"Someone has crossed the portal," said Miriam.

"Do you think that Costance has returned?" he asked.

"No," she answered. "It doesn't feel like that. But there are no Children in the corridor, so I cannot see from here." The two rose and went to the embarkation point.

In the long connecting tunnel between the docking portal and the main structure, Paul and Miriam saw two people walking toward them, a man and a woman.

"Citizen Explorers?" asked Paul.

"Be careful," said Miriam. Her face showed a deep-seated concern that Paul could not fully understand.

"Welcome to Galcon," he announced as he moved swiftly down the corridor to greet the couple.

"Where is Costance?" asked the woman.

Paul stepped back. He had not been given the name of the Ambassador before arriving on the planet. "Do you know him?" was all he could think of saying.

"You might say that," said the man. "We're here to recall him and authorize his return trip to earth. He and Vienna have been relieved of duty and may depart at any time."

Paul studied the two. He turned to Miriam. "They are closed to me," she said.

"The Ambassador has already left for earth," said Paul. The two passed knowing glances between them before Paul could continue. "But there is no safe way to get back to earth. I'm afraid that the Ambassador is dead. Vienna is dead too."

"Vienna dead?" said the woman. "I guess your life here won't be as entertaining as you thought, Blane."

"Still better than what we left," answered Wallerton. "At least we have citizens here to greet us." Turning to Miriam and Paul he said, "we have brought the transmission devices to restore the function of your Ceretraks."

Paul backed away as Miriam stepped forward to face them. "You'll find no one here who would use those devices," she said with a confidence that couldn't be doubted.

Paul took courage from her. "In any case," he added. "You will not be able to stay here. This place is about to pass away."

"And how would you know that? You are a *Discontinued*," said Quan with disgust.

"We are Sharers," said Miriam. "And we offer you your lives to come with us."

"No one is going anywhere," said Wallerton. "At least not until we've had a chance to discuss alternatives."

"You have no power in this place," said Paul in a matter-of-fact tone. "The only choice on this world is to trust the Children."

Mirabella turned to Wallerton, "Costance's last message said that these two were going native. Apparently he wasn't lying about that." Blane nodded agreement.

"Okay, we'll play your game," he said. "Just take us to the leader of the Photosynthoids."

Paul and Miriam called to the Children. "Do not be afraid," they answered. "Bring them to us. We stand at the high place."

"Very well," said Miriam. "We'll take you to the place where the Children wait for you." She turned and began to walk back down the corridor to the entrance of the main structure. Paul quickly followed. Cautiously, Quan and Wallerton joined the procession.

The four passed into the cross corridor that led to the atrium on the right, and to the ambassador's quarters on the left. They turned left and walked past the spot where Vienna had fallen. When they went by the open portal of Costance's apartments, Wallerton looked in and noticed the discarded handgun. "Wait a second," he commanded, disappearing into the room. He retrieved the automatic. "Buford always hedged his bets," he whispered to Quan.

"You'll find no good use for that," said Miriam. Quan and Wallerton made no answer.

Paul had been down this corridor before. It was here that he found the darkest time of his life. He remembered rushing headlong into that darkness. He had not remembered any portal or any awareness of when he had passed out of the crystalline structure and into the open air. Now he could see plainly the glistening pillars that marked the exit.

"Wait a minute," called Wallerton. "You're going to have to walk slower if you expect us to keep up with you in this darkness."

Miriam looked at Paul. It was the time of no shadows. They

could see the clear straight path leading up to the high place. With each step, Quan and Wallerton fell behind. They began to grope like children in a game of pin-the-tail-on-the-donkey.

"Go to the Children," said Paul to Miriam. "I will try to guide them as I was guided." He kissed her lightly and watched as she walked off in the sunlight. Paul turned back to Wallerton and Quan.

"Don't be afraid," he said, as he approached them.

"If this is some sort of trick, we don't think it is very funny," announced Quan.

"It is not a trick," said Paul calmly. "It is the darkness that you brought with you. You must pass through it to get to the high place."

"Where are you?" said Wallerton.

"I am right beside you," said Paul.

"How can you see?" asked Quan.

"I am not standing in the darkness," said Paul. "I will stay with you if you like. The important thing is to keep moving together. Take a step."

"Where? Which direction?" asked Wallerton.

"When you are at the center of the darkness," said Paul. "Any step is a step toward light."

"Cut the platitudes," barked Quan. "Do you think we won't

figure out this charade? When we do, you'll wish you hadn't been born."

"Take a step," urged Paul. The two moved tentatively. "You are doing fine, keep walking," he consoled.

"Where are you?" asked Wallerton. "Give me your hand."

"Would you take it?" asked Paul. He looked at the two. Blane Wallerton clutched at the gun.

"Yes," said Blane. "Mirabella and I will trust you to lead us through this."

"I can't lead you anywhere," stated Paul. "This darkness is a place in time. It is a place in your life that you must face to find your own way to the light. But, so that you may know that you are not alone, I will offer you my hand." He stretched out his arms and placed his right hand on Mirabella's shoulder and his left on Wallerton's. "You are not alone," he reiterated.

As if in unison, Wallerton and Quan swung to grab Paul. The hand that felt so solid in its kindness passed through them and their hands came up empty.

"Get down, Quan," commanded Wallerton. He raised the automatic and squeezed off every round in a circular arc trying to catch Paul. The cracking of the discharges seemed hollow and empty. The flashes of the muzzle offered no light to their darkness.

"Did you get him?" asked Quan.

"I can't tell," said Wallerton.

"I am here," said Paul. "And I will stay as long as you would like."

"We, sure as hell, don't need you," said Wallerton. "This fog will lift and you'll need the head start to get away from us."

"As you wish," agreed Paul. He turned his thoughts to the Children and to Miriam. He could see them off in the sunlight. Their song came strongly to his ears. The words invited them to the light. "I leave you to your darkness. Follow as you wish," he said with heaviness in his voice.

Paul began to walk away. Once, he looked back at the two companions. They were huddled together in the light, and they clutched each other for fear of the darkness. Ahead of him, Miriam spoke his name and he quickened his step.

31

As Paul approached the high place, Miriam rushed down to greet him. She took his hand as the two neared the edge of the plateau. Beyond was the great rift, the Valley of the Skree. The Children were in flight over the valley, and Paul and Miriam stood alone together.

"The Children say that the high place is a place for seeing," said Miriam. "I wish I could see more of what is in store for us."

"If Wallerton and Quan left earth knowing that they could never return, terrible things must be happening there," remarked Paul. "They would not relinquish their hold on earth so easily."

"The Children were not as closed off from their thoughts as we were," offered Miriam. "They now speak of the earth in images of destruction. They fear that no one will be left. In fact, they are beginning to call us the *safe ones*."

"Safe?" asked Paul. "Don't they also say that we cannot stay here. Don't they fear that their place is also in danger?"

"This is not our place," said the Children winging over the valley. "This place was established for your benefit. We have not been here for very long."

"Was the Ambassador right then?" Paul questioned. "He thought this whole planet could have been a space craft. He said that its sudden discovery in a place that had been empty indicated that it could be the Children's way to travel."

"His knowledge was incomplete," said the Children. "But he was right, in part. This is not our place. We have no place. You know us as the *Children*. We also call ourselves the *Travelers*. This is why we sing your song. It speaks to us. It was a great gift, Paul." As if on cue, the Children broke into the song:

185

Morning star and evening star,
shadows of light on light,
I walk a world of strangeness
and yet, I am at home.

The two humans joined in the singing, and Paul felt that his words were no longer strangers to himself. As abruptly as it began, the singing stopped. The Children spoke to the couple.

"It is time for you to become whole again," they said.

"What does that mean?" asked Paul.

Miriam spoke. "I think it means that we must go back into our bodies." Paul had forgotten that he was not within his own flesh. Now he was beginning to feel something. It was as if he were being pulled. At first it was a gentle tug. But a sudden sense of motion blurred his sight. He felt as though he were falling. His stomach was in his throat; his breath came in short gasps. Then everything was still. His breathing was calm and regular. He opened his eyes and saw the crystal dome overhead. He had fallen into his own body. He was lying on the divan in the place of healing. Miriam stirred next to him.

The two reached out to each other. The touch of her body felt the same as before, wondrous and familiar. At the foot of their resting place stood a Children.

"Our journey together will begin soon," said the Children. "I have been chosen to be with you. My name is Keeper."

"Your name?" questioned Miriam. "You have a name?"

"Yes," said Keeper. "I have been made the Keeper for your journey, and for a time, I will be disconnected. One day I may teach the Children what it is like to be alone."

"That is something I wish they never had to know," offered Paul.

"Where are the Children going," inquired Miriam, "that you will be alone?"

"They are not going away," answered Keeper. "They are going on, and I am staying with you. I will be the one who is away."

"Then you will be alone," said Paul, sadly.

The three of them heard the voice of all the Children saying, "The time is now complete." Quickly Keeper stepped up on the divan. He offered a webbed hand to Miriam and Paul, helping them to get up. The three stood together.

Keeper's extended wings encircled the two, protecting them as a mother hen brooding over her chicks. Light streamed on to the woman and the man from overhead. They looked up and saw the lower jaw and upward gaze of Keeper. They also saw, or felt, that they were growing larger, or the crystal dome was shrinking. In either case, the structure was encapsulating them.

They were in a sealed pod.

"Do not be afraid, Children," said Keeper. Miriam wondered if he were talking to them or to himself.

The ground began to shake. Before they could fear, however, the pod was lifted from the ground. Through the folds in the wings of the Photosynthoid, Miriam and Paul could see webbed fingers magnified through the prismatic sides of the pod.

"The Children are bearing us up!" exclaimed Miriam.

"The morning star and the evening star struggle to claim this place now that its time has ended," remarked Keeper. His simple words conveyed what Paul would later think of as a cosmic tug-of-war. The evening star pulled at the dense matter of the planet while the morning star stretched away the atmosphere. High in the sky, the pod slipped away with the excited gases that were being transformed into a hurling plasma of infinite power. In a breathtaking flash, the pod with the three passengers was hurtling among the stars. It was a darkness they had not seen in ages. The stars were sharp and clear and beautiful.

"Where are the Children?" gasped Miriam.

Floating beads of water splashed against the cheeks of Paul and Miriam. Keeper was weeping. He felt alone.

32

"Keeper, we are with you," said Paul

"I know you are, Child," said the Photosynthoid. "It is just that it is so quiet in my mind. I feel that you are close, but my seeing is alone."

"That is what we are like," answered Paul. "We see from one perspective, and we can shut out all other voices."

"How can you be so disconnected?" asked the creature.

"But we are connected," argued Paul. "That is what you taught us. It is our feelings that mislead us. We are never alone."

"Call to the Children," said Miriam.

"If they were here, I would know it," said Keeper. "It would be clear to me."

"All truth is not clear," observed Miriam. "Call to the Children. It may be that you will have to know them in another way."

In that confined space of isolation, three voices cried out as one. Beyond the translucent shell of the pod, in the deep cold of space, a light flared. At first it was one stream that paralleled their course, but soon it was joined by another and another.

"It is the Children," cried Miriam.

"The Travelers have joined us," observed Keeper. "They

lend us their light, and their light gives me hope."

It was true. The pod plummeted through the darkness of space, but it was surrounded by a cylinder of light. The forward edge of the tube expanded ahead of the craft while the tail end dimmed quickly. The Children were leaping ahead of the pod as quickly as it passed. They formed a circle of light, of light swifter than light.

Keeper began to sing.

> "With you are the fountains of life;
> in your light we see light."

Paul and Miriam found themselves without words, but wrapped in the joy of the moment and in the arms of each other.

In and out of days and weeks and, perhaps, years the three traveled together. If time was in that place at all, it could not have been measured. The three were Sharers, each giving life to the others. Always, the light of the Travelers fueled their hopes and gave Keeper the strength to freshen the air within and to provide *longstol*.

Paul and Miriam talked freely to one another. Keeper began to hear their voices as if they were the voices of the Children themselves.

"We are nearing our journey's end," he announced one day.

The words were incomprehensible to Paul. This way of being felt so right to him that he had forgotten the journey. Miriam was quicker to understand.

"Are we back at Earth?" she asked. The thought was frightening. In the safety of their crystal womb, the thought of reentering the world seemed an unnecessary hazard.

"We cannot stay here," said Keeper reading their thoughts. "You two must regain your place, and I, mine. The Travellers must take our new form. My skin begins to feel thin."

Miriam and Paul had no way to understand Keeper's words, but they awoke in darkness. The Children had gone.

"Are you alright, Keeper?" asked Miriam. "Where are the Children?"

"I am at peace, Daughter," said Keeper. "And the Children are near. The place of the morning sun is also near. You shall see it rise. It will be your first day." The words of Keeper seemed strange. Paul took note that never before had he referred to Miriam as *Daughter*. While they continued to wonder, Keeper withdrew his wings exposing the two to the panorama of empty space.

"Where are the stars?" asked Paul.

"Wait," said Keeper. Suddenly an arc of light defined the disk of a planet. It was a planet so close that it obscured all else from their field of view. In the center of the arc a ball of fluid fire emerged. It was the sun rising over the perimeter of the planet. In its new light, Paul and Miriam saw white clouds and blue seas. A shower of sparks flared in front of them.

"We must be hitting the outer atmosphere," observed Paul. He had no idea of how they could safely land, but he trusted Keeper.

The sparks became a steady glow, but the crystal sides of the pod felt cool to the touch. They were falling into the planet. There was no mistaking the increasing acceleration of their descent.

"Hold each other's hands," commanded Keeper. He didn't need to ask, for Paul and Miriam had joined hands in the anticipation of the moment. Keeper began to hum. The tone was deep and mysterious, but it rose slowly and deliberately. He was seeking a tone. When he matched that pitch, the pod joined in singing. All around Miriam and Paul were the harmonics of sound and light until, with a sudden burst, they were in free-fall. Rushing air screamed in their ears, and they locked hands tighter.

They felt themselves slowing down, as if reality had been usurped by a dream. The pressure of air against their entire bodies was replaced with tightness around their waists. Keeper had snatched them out of the air, and with his giant wings he soared earthward in ever widening circles. Paul and Miriam could see everything from their vantage point within the arms of Keeper.

Sights and smells came up to them, and like children, they shouted the name of each to the other.

"The sea, I smell the salt," cried Miriam.

"There's a gull," pointed Paul. They seemed like words from a deep memory or a life long forgotten. When Keeper alighted, the three fell exhausted to the ground.

"Remember when I asked to trade you for your feet?" said Paul. The three burst into laughter.

"Yes," said Keeper. "You were not able to keep your balance on the dunes, and you gave us your humor."

"And we have been in the pod so long that none of us has any legs worth trading for," said Paul, smiling at his two companions.

"Each day you two will grow stronger," offered Keeper. "You are the children of this place. It is right for you."

All during that first day it did seem right for Paul and Miriam. It was a lush place. A garden could not have provided more food, and the sounds of life were overwhelming.

"Keeper, you have found a wonderful place," said Miriam. "Can you hear the birds singing?"

"The Shadduah holds the sparrow," was Keeper's reply.

"And the Skree," responded Miriam. "We won't ever forget."

Mid-afternoon, Paul and Miriam fell asleep and did not stir until early evening. When they awoke, they had to remind each other of where they were.

"Where is Keeper?" asked Paul. The two called out in their minds for the Sharer, and saw him seated on a rock ledge near the ocean shore. They went to him. His skin seemed paler in the early evening light, more orange than green.

"Keeper, are you alright?" asked Miriam.

"Yes, Mother," he answered. Miriam looked to Paul.

"Do you want us to stay with you?" asked Paul.

"No," said Keeper. "I find joy in this place. And I find joy in being by myself at times, for I know that I am not alone."

"Call to us, we will be near," offered Paul.

"I want to watch the morning star set on a world where no evening star will rise," said Keeper. "Perhaps I will see my cousins among the stars," he added. After that, he kept silence.

The night air was cool, but Paul and Miriam slept warmly together on a bed of freshly cut grasses. When they awoke, they called to Keeper, but he did not answer. They went to the rock ledge and found his body. He looked as though he were sleeping peacefully.

"He had life, and he gave life," said Paul.

"And he was our Keeper," added Miriam. "Even now, the Shadduah holds him."

In unison, Paul and Miriam called out to the Children, and the Travelers were among them. They appeared as light within light, and a searing vision reflected off transformed faces. In the brightest of lights, Miriam and Paul saw Keeper arise, and spread his great wings. Their hearts were healed as they stood together.

In a moment, the brightness of Keeper's departure was replaced by clear blue skies and a wondrous sunshine. The only words Paul and Miriam heard that day came from their own lips.

"It is a wonderful place," said Miriam.

"Yes, it is," agreed Paul. The two walked together, and they were both naked, and they were not ashamed.

About the author:

Rob Smith is currently an Adjunct Instructor in Religion and Philosophy at Wright State University in Dayton, Ohio. There he has taught a popular course entitled "The Life, Religion, and Fiction of C.S. Lewis." Following the example of Lewis and Tolkien, his own fictional works are attempts to retell traditional myths in the form of popular fiction.

www.ingramcontent.com/pod-product-compliance
Lightning Source LLC
Chambersburg PA
CBHW020602250626
47154CB00004B/1331